EVACUATION
ORDER

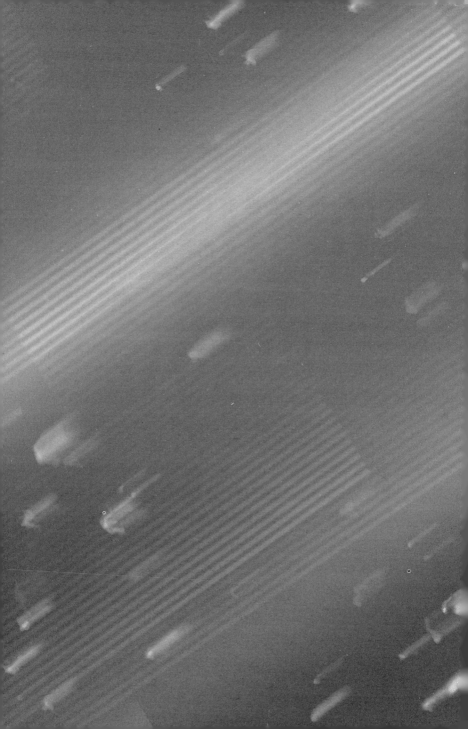

EVACUATION ORDER

JANE B. MASON AND
SARAH HINES STEPHENS

SCHOLASTIC INC.

Copyright © 2023 by Jane B. Mason and Sarah Hines Stephens

All rights reserved. Published by Scholastic Inc., *Publishers since 1920*. SCHOLASTIC and associated logos are trademarks and/or registered trademarks of Scholastic Inc.

The publisher does not have any control over and does not assume any responsibility for author or third-party websites or their content.

No part of this publication may be reproduced, stored in a retrieval system, or transmitted in any form or by any means, electronic, mechanical, photocopying, recording, or otherwise, without written permission of the publisher. For information regarding permission, write to Scholastic Inc., Attention: Permissions Department, 557 Broadway, New York, NY 10012.

This book is a work of fiction. Names, characters, places, and incidents are either the product of the author's imagination or are used fictitiously, and any resemblance to actual persons, living or dead, business establishments, events, or locales is entirely coincidental.

ISBN 978-1-338-62934-7

10 9 8 7 6 5 4 3 2 1   23 24 25 26 27

First edition, November 2023
Printed in the U.S.A. 40

Book design by Christopher Stengel

TO EVERYONE WHO HAS BATTLED A FOREST FIRE

CHAPTER
ONE

An eighteen-wheel semitruck rumbles down the California state highway, maintaining an easy speed. The driver sips coffee from a thermos mug—she is almost halfway through her twelve-hour shift and looking forward to delivering her load of farm equipment. Her first stop is a farm equipment warehouse in the Central Valley. After that, she'll head north to Mount Shasta to deliver the rest of the haul. Then it's just a few short hours on the road and she'll be home sweet home for several days of rest and family time.

The driver has been on the road for six weeks, and she is looking forward to meals that don't come in a bag, sitting on the sidelines at her kids' soccer games, and sleeping in her own bed.

Traffic slows slightly, and the driver downshifts, singing along to Bonnie Raitt. By the end of the song, traffic has smoothed out and the driver accelerates again. As the truck rounds a bumpy curve, a pair of chains hanging off the back of the trailer come loose, striking the pavement.

In the cab, the driver can't see or feel the loosened chains dragging behind the trailer. She takes another sip of coffee. The outside temperature has climbed to 98 degrees. This heat wave has lasted for over a week and she's grateful for her AC. Without it, she'd melt like a candle. Still, she'd rather drive in the heat than in snow or rain, even though she knows California could *really* use some precipitation. The dry, dry hills and seemingly endless drought are scary.

Pushing the thought from her mind, the driver slips into the passing lane and eases the semi past another big truck. As she moves back into the right-hand lane, a gust of wind kicks up a handful of tumbleweeds. Freed from their root stems, the round skeletons of desert plants bounce and roll across the highway, shaking loose and scattering seeds.

The soccer ball–sized tumbleweeds are tiny compared to the semi, and the truck rolls right over them. The spark that ignites one of the dry tufts when it meets the dragging chains is small, too. Too small for the driver to notice. But it is enough. The driver doesn't see the wisp of smoke, or the small flames that begin to crackle and grow. She continues down the highway with her load. The smoldering orbs drift onto the shoulder, where long-bladed clusters of dead grass have taken root. The tall, dry blades are exactly what the little fire needs to grow. Embers catch. Leap. Snap and sizzle.

Inside a Subaru several cars behind the truck, someone notices the fire growing on the side of the road and makes a 911 call.

CHAPTER
TWO

Right behind you!" Sam Durand calls to his best friend, Marco Nuñez. He pumps the pedals on his too-small Schwinn, hustling to keep up as the twosome roll out of town toward the Pacific Ocean. The bike ride to the beach is as familiar as their small town of Santa Bonita, though they don't get to the beach as often since school started up a little over a month ago. Sam feels his mood lighten as he pedals. He can feel the California sun on his back and the hot wind on his face. And best of all, though he can't see it yet, the Pacific Ocean is just over the horizon ahead of them.

A bead of sweat trickles down Sam's back. The hottest weather of the year comes late to their coastal village, making it feel more like summer than fall. The summer months along the Central Pacific

Coast are notoriously chilly, thanks to the layer of fog that rolls in for days at a time. September and October usher out the fog and bring the hotter temps, and this year those temperatures have been off the charts.

In spite of the heat, Sam is surprised by the lightness in his chest—a rare feeling for him. Since his dad died two years ago, October is almost always a long, hard slog of sadness and confusion. In a lot of ways, Nick Durand was gone before he was actually gone. In other ways, he wasn't. What lingers now are the memories—and the heavy way those memories make Sam feel.

But not today.

As he follows Marco to the base of the last hill, Sam feels so light that he might be able to fly. Grief is weird like that. Sometimes it presses down like a great weight. And sometimes it lifts—like the fog burning off at midday. Just evaporates. Sam doesn't know what makes some days harder and some days easier, but he'll take easier anytime he can get it.

Up ahead, Marco is starting up the hill. "You coming?" he shouts back, goading his friend just a little. Sam rises out of his seat, cursing the overstuffed pack on his back, and whizzes past Marco while he braces for the crushing 20 percent grade. They've ridden this hill hundreds of times, and every single climb brings burning legs and lungs.

"Dude!" Marco shouts, and gives chase.

Halfway up the hill, Sam is sucking wind. He opens his mouth to take a gulping inhale, and a massive horsefly zooms inside.

"Ugh, gross!" he shouts, spitting it out. The ejected fly—along with a hefty dose of spittle—is taken by the wind and splatters right onto Marco.

"Dude!" Marco pants in disgust as the hill levels off slightly before the final, steep ascent. "How many times do I have to remind you?! The *Rules for Biking* matter!" He rattles off the first few, landing heavily on rule number four. "Always, *always* look both ways before spitting!"

Sam shoots his friend a sideways glance. "You wanna talk about how you coughed a loogie on me last week? That was a million times grosser than a little spitty fly."

"A cough is involuntary!" Marco shoots back. "I had no control over that."

"And I can control a fly mistaking my tongue for a landing pad?" Sam rolls his eyes, laughing.

"You can control which way you spit, dude!"

Sam laughs through the panting. He can't argue with that. And it's hard to win with Marco—the kid always, always has a comeback.

"Race you to the top," Sam shouts, changing the subject. The grade is steeper now, and they are closing in on the crest of the hill. On the other side, the blue of the Pacific Ocean stretches as far as the eye can see. They can already hear it . . . even over their labored breathing.

Marco passes Sam on the left, pumping hard. Sam sprints as fast as he can, pulling up alongside his friend thirty feet from the top.

Side by side, the boys struggle their way to the summit.

"You got this," Marco calls, inching ahead, and then adds, "unless I get it first!"

Sam saves his breath and puts everything he has into his legs to keep pace with his friend. He could complain that his bike is smaller, but Marco would just ignore him.

The two boys crest the hill at the same time and roll to a stop at the ocean overlook, gasping for air. Sam's lungs are on fire, but it is so worth it. The blue sky is dotted with puffy white clouds, and the ocean's surface sparkles a deep, almost metallic blue in the afternoon sun. The boys sip from their water bottles and stare out, the breeze drying the sweat under their T-shirts.

"Dude," Marco says again. Anyone else might think Marco is about to add another word. Sam, though, knows exactly what he means. For the two of them, *dude* is not just one word—it's practically a whole language. Depending on the inflection, *dude* can be a taunt, an agreement, or a question. Right now it simply means "wow."

"Dude," Sam agrees with a nod as they gaze out. The view is spectacular.

"Hey, look." Marco points at a single pelican gliding on the air current just below the boys, watching for fish. The bird dives but comes up empty, then with two easy flaps rises higher into the sky until it is eye level with the boys. They've seen lots of birds here before, but pelicans are a bit unusual. "There must be some kind of fish run along the coast," Marco says. Another pelican swoops in, and then a third, making a trio, and together they flap higher into the sky, moving in synchronicity.

Sam swallows as he watches the birds make their way north along the coast, feeling the familiar October heaviness returning. He used to be part of a trio, too. The three pelicans fly close to one another in a V formation, drifting easily on the air currents. When they finally disappear from view, Sam's gaze drops to the shoreline, to the waves rolling in. Day and night, in any kind of weather—in stormy and calm waters—the patterns of the Pacific remain constant. The tide comes in; the tide goes out. And then it comes in again. It always returns. Sam closes his water bottle and searches desperately for the lightness he'd felt earlier. His chest only tightens. The tide always returns, but his father never will.

THREE

Sam steps away from the edge of the little cliff and forces himself into action. They can't stand around looking at the ocean all day . . . they have work to do. More specifically, they have photos to take.

"You ready?" he asks, dropping his bike next to a huge patch of ice plant.

"I was born ready," Marco replies with a smirk.

Rolling his eyes, Sam unshoulders his backpack and pulls out the old plaid blanket he's been carrying around all day. He starts down the narrow path that leads to the beach, with Marco at his heels. Once they hit the sand, Sam takes several long minutes to lay the blanket out, stepping back to look at it, then tugging here and there. He has to get everything just right. He pulls a corner, and then goes back and rumples up a couple of other areas. Marco watches patiently, his arms folded across his chest, his head cocked to the side so that a lock of black hair flops in his face. Sam knows what's coming.

"Dude. I think you missed a wrinkle." Marco lifts one eyebrow. His brown eyes twinkle.

"It's got to be right," Sam replies, so busy studying the blanket that he doesn't see Marco mouthing those exact words at the same time. Marco shakes his head slightly and puffs air out of his nose. After more than a year, it's getting harder to find the humor in this whole thing. It has been a long road of strictly staged photos, and there doesn't appear to be an end in sight.

Finally, Sam pulls a camera case out of his backpack and unzips it. He cradles the vintage Nikon as he carefully unwraps the soft piece of flannel—cut from one of his dad's old shirts—that he keeps around the camera for extra measure.

"Ready?" he asks.

"I repeat," Marco says. "Born."

"Okay, sit here . . ." Sam points to a particular place on the blanket before removing a photograph from an envelope in his backpack, being careful not to bend it. It's black and white, and shows a woman on a beach—this beach—sitting on a blanket—the blanket Sam just spread on the sand. He shows the photo to Marco so he can see what they're after.

Marco sighs. "Just tell me what you want me to do," he says, easing himself onto the blanket like an old man. He puts his hands down first, going into a weird-looking downward dog, then rotates his body around slowly. He has learned the hard way not to mess up a blanket (or any other prop carefully situated by Sam) before the camera clicking begins.

Sam sets the photo on his backpack and looks back at Marco, then the photo, then Marco. "Turn your torso toward the water," he directs, "and lift your chin a little." He brings the viewfinder to his eye and adjusts the aperture. "Turn a little bit more, and rest your hand on your thigh.

"Not like that," he says. "Make it look natural."

Marco rolls his eyes but says nothing . . . he knows better. He's been through this fifty thousand times. Taking photos several days a week is part of a project—an obsession—that Sam has been working on for over a year. Sam is re-creating his dad's photographs as closely as he can, using the same props, the same spaces, and looking through the same lens. The only difference between his father's photos and Sam's is that Marco is the model in every single one.

Sam's dad, Nick Durand, was a professional photographer just beginning to catapult to fame when he died. He was known for his evocative images—stark and haunting pictures that suggest an entire story. He shot everything with an old-fashioned film camera—never digital. And he developed every one of his own prints.

Sam barks out a few more instructions and Marco complies, his humor fading. He's not in the mood for this right now, but knows that this project matters to Sam more than his friend can explain. He's chasing something big with every click of the shutter. Marco wants to help, but he's burnt out. Whatever his friend is looking for, he hopes he finds it soon.

Sam clicks and clicks and clicks. A tiny smile tugs at the corners of his mouth as it begins to feel almost . . . right. They are in exactly the right place, with the right blanket (his mother never throws anything away). The afternoon light is that soft pink his father always loved.

"Drop your chin," Sam says. "There. Perfect." Several more clicks and Sam finally lowers the camera from his face. He thinks he's nailed it, but he can never be sure until the prints are made . . . and sometimes not even then.

Marco heaves a sigh. His arm is cramping. "Dude," he breathes. And what he means is "mercy."

"I think that's good," Sam says at last, granting his friend a reprieve. "But I won't know until later."

Marco gets to his feet, shakes out his stiffening limbs, and brushes the sand off his hands. "As I believe I've suggested ten thousand times, using your camera phone would tell you right away whether you'd—"

"And as I've told you ten thousand times, I can't use a digital camera because my father didn't." Sam's expression shifts subtly at the mention of his father.

Marco, who can read his friend as easily as his favorite graphic novel, raises his hands in surrender. "Never mind! Delete that from the record!" Marco will do anything to preserve Sam's good mood. A cheerful Sam is as rare as California rain! "Am I fired?" Marco asks, eyebrows launching skyward.

Sam shakes his head and laughs. "Dude! Of course not. Who else would I get at your rate?"

Marco clucks his tongue as he lifts the blanket, being careful not to shake sand anywhere near the camera. He's been trained to protect that thing with his life. "If you think I'm doing this for free, you're sadly mistaken. I'll take today's payment in frozen custard."

Sam rewraps the camera and zips it safely back into its case, chuckling. Marco is no pushover. By the time he has everything shoved back into his pack, Marco is racing up the path to their bikes.

"Let's see if you and your tiny bike can keep up with me!" he shouts over his shoulder.

Sam slips his arms through both straps of his backpack as he runs to catch up. Lifting the bike he outgrew at least two years ago, he throws a leg over the bar. Marco pushes off first and Sam jealously eyes his best friend's ancient but proper-size Huffy. The bike is a workhorse. Half the letters are scratched off—only *FFY* are still visible, and Marco has turned the second *F* into an *L*.

"Watch me flyyyyyyy!" he calls over his shoulder as he picks up speed. The chase is on.

FOUR

The whisper of burning weeds transforms into a murmuring roar as more and more dry grass and tangled tumbleweeds ignite and the fire extends along the side of State Highway 21. Sparks pop and fly through the air in multiple directions. They land on small piles of leaves, sticks, grass, and dead branches. *Whoosh!* The hungry fire eats them all, crackling with every gust of wind.

Fifteen miles away, an alarm sounds in CAL FIRE's Northwood Forest Station. The on-duty crew deserts their late lunch, running for their fire suits and engines.

The hard, cold truth is that Sam can't keep up with Marco on a downhill. It is all about physics. His bike wheels are just too small. Plus, Marco is bigger, which gives him another edge—weight advantage. Still, Sam tries, pumping so hard the bike wobbles as he picks up speed.

"I'm right behind you, Superman," Sam calls. "Better not get tangled in your cape."

They roar over the first roll of the hill and into the steeper section at the bottom, descending into the little valley. The stoplight at the edge of the village changes to green as they turn in to the small downtown—their favorite timing. Marco lets out a little whoop and rolls through the intersection without braking.

As soon as the boys cross the Bay Street intersection, they are officially back in the village. Settled during the gold rush, Santa Bonita is loved by locals and a steady stream of loyal tourists willing to exit the highway and traverse the winding roads to get to the geographical gem. Santa Bonita, or Saint Beautiful, is a sampler pack of California's greatest hits: ocean beaches, redwood groves, rugged hills, and scenic vistas tucked along the meandering coast.

Just six blocks long, Main Street Santa Bonita is made up mostly of old, two-story wood and brick buildings. Larger, more commercial developments have been kept to the outskirts, like the hospital where Sam's mother works, which is east of the village, on the other side of Maybeck Ridge along with Home Depot and Target.

Sam keeps up his pedaling, and thanks to inertia, he swerves by his best friend, taking the lead just as they pass the post office. They roll by the bakery, the two-screen movie theater, the hardware store, and Green Owl Grocery—not quite a supermarket but perfect for putting together your beach picnic or grabbing local produce—where Marco pulls back in front. They leapfrog like this all the way to Inside Scoop, where Marco brakes hard, swinging his back tire around and screeching to a stop. He is practically through the door before Sam has even swung off his Schwinn.

The familiar tinkling of the bell on the door announces the boys' arrival in what is probably their favorite spot in town. Inside Scoop has been around almost as long as Santa Bonita itself. The ice cream shop has passed from generation to generation and has also kept the owner, Esther Hightower, working long past retirement age. When she hears the bell, Esther looks up and greets the boys the way she always does in the late afternoon.

"Dessert before dinner *again*?" she singsongs, smiling brightly and loading a giant carton of rocky road into one of the freezers. Her wispy gray hair is pulling out of the braided bun she wears high on her head, giving her a frizzy hair halo. Her blue eyes twinkle.

"Por supuesto," Marco replies.

"Well, thank goodness." Esther winks back. "Gives me job security."

In the summer, when Santa Bonita is flooded with tourists, the line for a custard cone can stretch halfway down the block . . . not unlike the line of traffic trying to leave town on those same dog days of summer. The single road out can get clogged with sand-covered, sunburned tourists pretty easily. In the off season, though, things slow way down and the small business owner is grateful for the after-school crowd that makes up the majority of her business.

Esther pulls a pair of sugar cones from a giant box and the ice cream scoop from a bowl of milky-looking water. She serves up two scoops of chocolate for Sam, and then a double peanut butter for Marco. Yesterday, Marco was first. Esther knows her regulars.

"Thanks, Esther. Thanks, dude," Marco says, licking his dripping cone while Sam pays.

"Say hello to your families, and make sure you don't melt out there in that heat," Esther calls as the boys head back outside.

Even without AC, it's cooler in the shop because of the freezers, but both Sam and Marco would rather sit outside and try to catch a breeze.

They're settled on the bench outside and licking their drippy cones when Hank Jones comes out of the hardware store, keys jangling. He waves at the boys and locks the door to his shop.

Sam checks his watch. In Santa Bonita, everyone knows everyone *and* their business. It's early for the hardware store to close.

Hank passes the boys on the way to his parked truck—an impeccable 1960s Chevy. The truck is Hank's pride and joy; its blue paint is almost as fresh as the day he bought it. "Dessert before dinner again?" Hank jokes, raising an eyebrow.

"Good one, Hank!" Marco replies with a laugh. Both he and Esther say this every single time they see them eating ice cream in the afternoon, but the boys don't mind. It's comforting, actually.

Hank opens his truck door with a key and shakes his head. "Someday I'll come up with another joke and you two won't know what to do." He chuckles. "Until then . . . save room for dinner!"

Sam's smile fades as he watches Hank climb into the cab. Is he moving more slowly than usual? Did he wince when he put his weight on his left leg? Seems like it, but Sam can't be sure. This is a habit he has developed since his dad died . . . watching people, wondering if they're okay. Worrying.

Marco's cone is gone before Sam's, like always, and he licks the last sticky bits off his fingers while Sam finishes. When both cones are gone, the boys wave to Esther through the gingham curtains and roll toward home. Their competitive edges are dulled by cream and sugar and they ride down Main Street side by side, enjoying the late-afternoon breeze. Sam is pedaling easily, when his nose begins to twitch and he inhales more deeply. He smells smoke, and it's not the kind that comes from the diner or the barbeque grill that's sometimes set up outside the Sand Bar. No, this is something else. Then he remembers: It's fire season. It comes every year, like Halloween or Christmas, only without candy or presents, just orangey brown sunsets, lots of news reports, and a general sense of doom.

Sam pedals a little harder, trying to shake off the heaviness threatening like a storm cloud. Fire season is just a bummer, he tells himself. It's not a big deal.

CHAPTER
SIX

Woof!" Goodboy is at the door before Sam even has his hand on the knob. He flings the door open and drops to the floor to greet his dog.

"It's me!" Sam calls out to his mom while the rescued pit bull waggles wildly, trying to land his tongue on Sam's face. Of all the things Sam's mom did to cheer him up after his dad died, adopting a dog has worked the best. "I missed you, too, GB," Sam says. The last of his threatening worry cloud evaporates while the pup licks every inch of his cheeks . . . and chin . . . and forehead. With that daily task accomplished, Goodboy sits back on his hind legs and radiates love.

"Sorry I'm late," Sam calls out again—to both GB and his mom. He is responsible for Goodboy and can tell with a quick glance at the dog bowls that his mom has already fed him.

Sam's mom, Vivian, doesn't seem to mind his tardiness. "He's been stationed by the door all afternoon!" she says, laughing as she comes into the kitchen. Vivian is ready for work, dressed in printed scrubs and bright red clogs, her dark curly hair pulled back from her face. Today's scrubs have octopuses all over them—she likes to pick prints that will bring some cheer to the young patients she often works with. "I think GB misses your summer schedule," she adds.

Goodboy is flopped on the floor now, his paws in the air, officially asking for a tummy rub. Sam reaches over and gives him a massive, belly-covering massage.

"Me too, GB. Me too," he tells the pup. "I'd choose our lazy days over school and homework anytime!"

Sam's mom is nodding. "I'm sure you would, but you know the drill while I'm at work. Homework first! I left some meat loaf in the fridge for dinner, and there's a bag of peas in the freezer."

Sam is only half listening—he's been getting the same instructions every afternoon for six weeks now. Plus, he's anxious to get to the darkroom to see how his shots came out. Still, he tries to cool his jets. This little afternoon window is the only time he and his mom have together since she switched to the night shift at the hospital, and he did take his time getting home. Neither of them likes this situation, but the night shift pay is better, and they need the money to make ends meet without his dad.

"I think I got the perfect lighting for dad's Halcyon Beach shot,"

Sam says without thinking. He always feels a little sheepish bringing the project up . . . he knows his mom isn't psyched about it, even though she would never say it out loud. Vivian smiles at him in response, but it's not her old smile . . . it's the fake-it-until-you-make-it smile she concocted to make him feel half-okay after his dad died.

Sam tells himself that it's okay that she doesn't understand how much he truly needs this project. He's not even sure *he* understands why he needs it. He tells himself it's enough that she helps him pay for film—which isn't cheap—and keeps his dad's old darkroom up and running for him to use. A part of Sam wishes she wanted to talk about it, though. She seems to avoid bringing it up or asking how it's going.

Watching her face now, with that weird smile, Sam's shoulders slump a tiny bit. These early-evening handoffs make him lonely before he's even alone. Goodboy is excellent company, but the house feels empty without his mom in it.

And sometimes when she's home, he thinks. The words *I miss you* pop into his head. Sam almost says them out loud before stopping himself. It's weird, but a lot of the time he misses his mom even more than he misses his dad. And his dad is the one who is actually gone.

"Call the Nuñezes if you need anything, okay?" his mom is saying—more instructions he knows by heart. "And don't forget to turn off the oven." Her words will continue to echo even in her absence.

She's with me, Sam tells himself, *she's still here. It's enough.* It has to be, because it's what they have.

Sam's mom grabs her purse, and the sweater she always takes for the over-air-conditioned hospital, off the hook by the door. "I'll try to check in with you later," she says. "And will definitely see you in the morning!" She gives him a quick hug—they are the same height now. Then she's gone.

Sam stares at the curtain covering the window on the front door, watching it flutter and then resettle. Goodboy paws his leg, bringing him back to reality. "Dinner and homework can wait, boy," Sam says aloud. "I've got shots to develop!"

In the complete dark of the darkroom, Sam takes a breath before getting to work. He loves it in here . . . loves the quiet darkness. It's the place where he feels closest to his dad . . . maybe even closer than he felt when he was alive.

He cracks open the canister with a satisfying pop and unrolls the film in a long strip. After snipping it free with scissors, he rolls it onto the reel and drops the whole thing into the film tank. Once the tank's lid is snapped shut, he takes another breath before turning the lights back on.

After that, it's a process of mixing the chemicals to develop the film, agitating everything, and timing the stop bath. He goes through these motions almost automatically now, hardly thinking of the first few times he tried to develop film on his own. So many failed attempts! How many times had Marco asked why the heck he wanted to spend his time in the dark instead of heading to the beach or playing video games? So many.

Marco's voice echoes in his head now . . . *Dude, you're going to turn into a mushroom!*

Finally (finally!), Sam completes the last step in developing, and he can rinse his negatives and hang them to dry.

Sam startles when he hears a sound outside the door. Goodboy has learned that Sam is off-limits when he's in the darkroom, but sometimes he just can't help himself. There's a second scratch at the door, followed by a whimper.

"Almost done, boy!" Sam calls as he hangs the last negative. "Time for *my* dinner," he adds, stomach growling.

Standing in the kitchen a few minutes later, Sam wishes he'd thought to put the meat loaf in the oven *before* going into the darkroom. They don't have a microwave, so he opts for the pan-on-the-stove method. He tries to take his time—he can't make his prints until the negatives are completely dry anyway—but his whole body is tingling with anticipation. He. Just. Can't. Wait. To. See. The. Shots!

Goodboy gives another whimper when Sam disappears back into the darkroom. "I'll try to be quick!" Sam assures him, though he knows it's an empty promise. Making prints is tedious and difficult, and he often spends hours reprinting a single image. Plus, sometimes just seeing the photos slices him open like a filleted trout.

Today is a slicing day. As images begin to appear on the paper in the dim red light, a lump forms in Sam's throat. Within seconds, tears gather in the corners of his eyes. The darkroom is the only place Sam allows himself to cry. He hasn't in almost a week, but today the tears are determined. Grief is sneaky like that. Besides the tidal ebbing and flowing, there are sometimes massive sneaker waves that come out of nowhere and knock you down and drag you over rough sand. Sam tries to see the print in the developer bath but can't through his tears. He pulls it too late. Sighing, he gets another sheet of photo paper and starts again. He wonders if his dad is watching, shaking his head at the son who never gets it right on the first try.

The truth is, Sam's dad was gone long before he died. When his photography career began to take off, around the time Sam was in second grade, Nick spent more time traveling than he spent at home . . . a lot more. And then, when Sam was nine, his father was diagnosed with cancer. The traveling came to a screeching halt, but the leaving never stopped. Nick was home full-time then, but without a moment for Sam. The chemotherapy treatments were awful. His dad was always either exhausted or angry. Or both. And the whole time his mom was a sad, worried mess.

Then, after eight months of agony, Sam's dad left them for good.

CHAPTER

SEVEN

As the sun rises, the growing fire moves up an unburned hillside. There is plenty of fuel to feed its ravenous hunger in the undeveloped area—too much, in fact. Dying brush, fallen branches, and dropped leaves have accumulated and become bone dry in the drought. The fire consumes them quickly and pushes on.

For decades it was assumed that the safest thing to do when wildfires started was to extinguish them as quickly as possible. But in the years before that, when Native Americans were stewards of the land, they had a different understanding of land management. They felt it was important to let some fires burn and regularly scorched the earth, often intentionally, to clear the brush, branch, and leaf fall. To them, fire was a part of the forest ecosystem. They knew that small burns both cleared and fertilized the land. When flames are never allowed to flicker, forests become clogged with debris, so that when a fire starts, it quickly becomes an insatiable inferno that gobbles everything in its path. Now out of control, the once-useful fire becomes intensely destructive.

A light but steady wind stirs as the day stretches on. It pushes the fire onward, adding oxygen to the dangerous mix. The fire grows stronger and hotter, moving faster and faster.

A few miles away, a doe and her fawn pause in their early-morning browsing and raise their heads. Their dark noses quiver, alert to approaching danger.

EIGHT

Stripes of sunlight fall on Sam's wall, streaming through the window blinds. After tossing and turning all night, he's glad to see the sun in the sky, but the light coming in his window is unusual. It's hazy, a little orange, and a *lot* eerie. He climbs out of bed without waking GB, who is dreaming in his donut bed beside Sam's twin. Sam flips the light switch to try to erase the spooky glow before it colors his mood, but it's already too late. He sniffs. Smoke. There is definitely smoke blowing in from a forest fire not too far away.

Ah, the sights and smells of fire season! Marco's voice is right there in Sam's head, giving even this a sarcastic take, brushing it off.

Downstairs, Sam finds his mom at the kitchen counter, drinking tea and gazing out the window. Her hair has been released from its barrette and falls to her shoulders. Her octopus scrubs are rumpled. Sam is really happy to see her doing what she always does after getting home from work. "How was your night?" he asks.

Vivian turns toward him, and Sam sees that her eyes are kind of red. Has she been crying?

Sam can count on one hand the number of times he has seen his mom cry. Three of those times were right after his dad died. He wonders about this a lot. Is she putting on a brave face? Is it for him? Does she cry when she's alone in her car? Or has she used up all her tears? It all seems possible.

"Work was okay," she replies, sounding distracted as she takes another sip from her mug. Sam isn't convinced. He opens the back door and steps out onto the small deck, where they have a café table with chairs and a gas grill. The smoky smell is stronger outside. The sky in the distance looks heavy and sort of brownish . . . like he's peering through layers of smoke. To see any blue at all, he has to look straight up, and even then the sky seems faded and dingy.

"Where's the fire?" Sam asks, stepping back into the kitchen. Goodboy is on his heels, and Sam pours a scoop of kibble into his bowl. His mom doesn't want to talk about the fire, but he *does*.

Vivian Durand sets her tea down before answering. "Near Scottstown. You need to leave for school soon. Are you going to have a bowl of cereal?"

"Is it big?" Sam asks.

Before his mom can answer, the *whop whop whop* of a helicopter echoes over the house. The sounds of fire season have arrived along with the sights and smells.

His mom gets out a bowl, the milk, and a couple of cereal choices and puts them on the table. "You need to eat something," she says. With a sigh, Sam sits down and fills a bowl with store-brand Crispy Rice. His mom gives a small nod, as if satisfied. "I'm going to shower," she says. "Don't forget to pack your homework. Oh, and can you make sure all of the windows are closed before you go? The air quality isn't great today."

So the fire is big enough to make it hard to breathe, Sam thinks as she leaves the room. He eats quickly, washes his bowl, and sets it to dry in the drainer. He checks all the windows in the house, his breath getting shallower as he thinks about the toxins that must be floating around in the air, just waiting for an opportunity to get into his lungs. There was a time when he had no idea what an air quality index was, but thanks to fire season, he is fully aware that an AQI over 100 is unhealthy.

Sam is double-checking that all the windows are latched when a hand on his shoulder makes him jump.

"Try to think positive," his mom says. "It's going to be fine, Sammy." Her hair is wet from the shower, and the citrus smell of her shampoo masks the smoke for a brief moment.

Sam plasters on his own fake smile. Of all the words in the English language, he hates *fine* the most. *Fine* is never fine.

"They'll get it contained," his mom continues.

Sam tries to swallow away the tickle in his throat. He's afraid if he speaks, his voice will betray him. The only thing worse than worrying is when his mom worries about his worrying! He's beyond grateful when Marco walks in with a resounding "Dude!"

For the past two years, and even before that, Sam and Marco have been treating each other's homes like their own. On any given day, you might see Marco with his nose in the Durand pantry, or Sam with his back end poking out of the Nuñezes' refrigerator. They each have regular seats at the other's family table. Knocking was abandoned long ago.

Goodboy bounds over and gives Marco a warm, wet welcome while Sam swallows and chokes out a "Dude!" of his own.

"You should see the smoke rising over Box Canyon!" Marco scratches GB's velvety soft ears. Marco sounds kind of exhilarated, but it doesn't mitigate Sam's mounting concerns.

"Is Box Canyon closer than Scottstown?" he asks.

Sam looks from Marco to his mom and sees them exchange a look of their own. It's a look that Sam knows a lot better than he'd like to—the one they use to caution each other about Sam's "fragile state." Sam hates that look almost as much as he hates the word *fine*. He decides not to wait for an answer. Instead, he grabs his lunch from the refrigerator, pushes Marco back out the door he just came through, and calls a quick goodbye to his mom and GB. He takes the stairs down to the driveway two at a time.

"Race you to school!" he yells, changing the subject and, he hopes, his mood.

CHAPTER

NINE

Sam and Marco are both out of breath when they roll up to the Upper School building at Buena Vista Elementary School. They rode the near-daily route faster than usual, and instead of needing to race to class like they often do, they have a minute to pause and take in the ocean view the school is named for as they lock their bikes. "It's not such a buena vista when you look this way," Marco jokes, staring at the school entrance with his back to the Pacific.

Sam manages a "Ha," but his heart isn't in it. His jackrabbit brain, which likes to jump from one worry to the next, has landed squarely on concerns over their fast ride, the air quality, and the effects of exercising in smoke. Is the bad air to blame for their breathlessness? Shouldn't he have caught his breath by now?

"Is the smell getting stronger?" Sam asks as they walk to the banks of lockers located in a breezeway that cuts through the middle of the building. Sam sniffs the collar of his shirt. Maybe the smell is in his clothes. Maybe it's stuck in his nose.

"Oh, you are *definitely* smelling stronger!" Marco laughs and waves his hand in front of his nose.

"Are you talking about the smoke?" Elsie Williams asks. She has a locker right between Marco's and Sam's, which is very convenient since she's their next-best friend. All three have been in the same class since kindergarten, and Sam can't imagine Buena Vista without either of them. "I definitely think the smell is getting stronger," Elsie confirms. She nods at Sam with a wrinkled brow—concern is clear in her green eyes before she turns and rolls them at Marco, lightly elbowing him out of the way so she can access her locker. Not everything is a joke.

Lockers slam in quick succession and the three friends join the stream of seventh graders making their way to Mr. Billings's humanities room.

Just before they get to the door, Marco pulls on Sam's arm. Sam turns and Marco looks him dead in the eye. "Dude?" he asks.

"I'm not freaking out," Sam insists as they walk into class. "I'm just curious."

"Ah, curiosity! It's good to stay curious!" Mr. Billings overhears the boys talking and cannot help but chime in when he hears a favorite word. "Curious about what?" he asks as the students settle in.

"We're just wondering what's going on with this fire." Elsie's voice is so low it's practically a growl. She is by far the shortest kid in the class, but you'd never guess it by the sound of her.

"Do they even know how the fire started?" Kim Lee asks from the back row.

"Or how they're going to put it out?" Sarah Jennings adds.

Mr. Billings nods his head, looking thoughtful. The bearded teacher is fairly new to the school but has quickly become one of Sam's favorites. Sam likes the way he listens to his class and encourages conversations, asking just the right questions, so that when you arrive at an answer, it feels as though you figured it out yourself and weren't spoon-fed it by the teacher.

Still nodding, Mr. Billings picks up an eraser and wipes the big whiteboard at the front of the room, erasing the previous day's writings. In humanities they talk about lots of things, including current events, and this fire is feeling like an event.

"Okay, let's start at the start," he says.

FIRE CAUSES, he writes. "How do we think they start?"

Hands shoot up. Mr. Billings calls on one person at time while a girl named Elisabeth Olsen records the answers.

HUMANS/ACCIDENT
   campfire
   matches/cigarettes
   fireworks
LIGHTNING

SUN/HEAT
HUMANS/ARSON

When Mr. Billings calls on Kylie Burke, she has a comment. "It seems like the fires are getting worse every year, though, doesn't it? Is that because of climate change? Is that another human cause of fire?"

Marco looks at Sam and Elsie and nods. "Looks like we've got a beard-stroker," he whispers.

As if on cue, Mr. Billings sets down the marker and puts his palm to his beard, his telltale sign for a pause and a think.

Elsie snorts out a laugh, and Sam's lips curve into a tiny smile, but he isn't really that amused. In fact, the class conversation is making him more anxious, not less.

"Climate change, the drought, higher temperatures, and shifting seasons—yes, those are all things that can cause fires to grow bigger and happen more frequently. But they don't *start* the fires, so maybe these things belong in a different category?" Mr. Billings suggests.

"Right, like . . . challenges?" Elsie chimes back in.

Mr. Billings nods. He tells Elisabeth to start a second list beside the first and asks if anyone else can think of things that might make a fire harder to fight. Terrain and size of the fire are added to the board. Then Eric Martinez, who has never been seen without a soccer ball, suggests wind.

"Yes!" Mr. Billings nods vigorously and starts explaining with his hands *and* his words. "The Diablo and Santa Ana winds are notoriously hot and gusty. They come streaming down from the Sierra mountain ranges and cross the Central Valley at the end of the dry season, right when seasonal lightning storms are starting." He turns to the board. "Add the winds together with the sparks and you have the perfect recipe for fire disaster." His voice booms in exclamation before he turns back to his students. Seeing their faces, his own face falls and he goes back to stroking his beard.

This new understanding of fire is not settling anyone's nerves. Eric's eyes are as big as his soccer ball. Elsie clears her throat, and when she speaks again Sam can hear that her voice has gone up an octave. Kylie is grabbing the bathroom pass from its hook by the door and heading into the hall. Even Marco can't stop jiggling his foot.

The teacher looks at Sam, who is picking the skin around his fingernails.

Sam can feel Mr. Billings's eyes on him but cannot raise his head to meet his favorite teacher's gaze.

CHAPTER
TEN

When the bell rings for lunch, Sam silently congratulates himself for keeping his cereal down for three whole periods. At the same time, he isn't at all sure how the leftover meat loaf is going to sit, or if he can manage to even get it down. His stomach is doing cartwheels.

It's okay. I'm okay, he tells himself as he walks down the hall. *Not fine . . . but okay.*

Before they left humanities, Mr. Billings reminded the class that there are emergency crews trained to fight fires. CAL FIRE is 100 percent dedicated to combating forest fires in California, and professional firefighting crews often come in from out of state to lend a hand.

"They know what they're doing. They are trained professionals, and their job is to protect us." Mr. Billings's parting words echo in Sam's head.

And they didn't talk about the fog or other aspects of weather or climate that might be helpful in containing fires . . . especially this close to the coast. Santa Bonita village has never had a big fire come through before, and that's due in large part to the coastal moisture that usually helps keep things in check. Sam considers this comforting thought as he approaches his regular lunch table, where his friends await.

"Dude," Sam says, cueing Marco to slide over and make room on the cafeteria bench, which he quickly does.

"Dude," Marco returns the greeting with a slight lift of his chin.

Elsie, sitting opposite, rolls her eyes. "Dudes," she rumbles.

Sam unpacks his apple and container of meat loaf. He sets them on the table, stares at them, and waits for Marco to start up with his usual distracting blather. Marco, though, is surprisingly quiet.

Elsie notices, too. "Hey, are you okay?" she asks after ten minutes have passed and their chattiest friend is still not talking. A silent Marco is downright troubling.

"Just thinking." Marco shakes his head.

"Okaaaay." Elsie sounds skeptical as she shoves the last bite of sandwich into her mouth. "I have a *Buena Vista Bugle* meeting," she says. Sam remembers it's Wednesday, when the school paper meetings are held. "You want my brownie?" Elsie holds it out to Marco, who shakes his head.

"Suit yourself," Elsie says, shrugging. "I'll see you guys later."

As Elsie walks away, Sam studies his friend. Is Marco thinking the same thing Sam is thinking? Is he making a mental list of WHAT COULD GO WRONG? Has he included NOT ENOUGH FIREFIGHTERS and HURRICANE FORCE WINDS? Not that there are actual hurricane force winds happening right now . . . But seeing a glum Marco is as unsettling as the smell of smoke in the air. Maybe more so.

Sam bites into his apple and takes out his phone to search for something, anything, to get their minds off fire.

He opens the photo tab and scrolls. While Sam would never use his phone to take the photos he stages and shoots, he *does* use it to take reference shots of the photos he wants to re-create and to track progress on the overall project. He happily moves yesterday's beach shot to the finished folder (all those extra hours in the darkroom were worth it!). He clicks through pictures he still wants to take, until he comes across one his dad shot in a secluded redwood stand between his house and Marco's, a place the boys have gone to countless times. It's perfect!

Sam leans toward Marco to show him. "Let's do this one today, okay? Right after school?" The photo project never fails when Sam needs a distraction. He figures it probably works the same way for his number one (and only) model, too. Marco doesn't look up from his phone, but at least he nods. Sam leans a little closer to try to see what's holding Marco's attention, but the boy tilts the phone away. All Sam can see is a flash of a map with little flame icons on it . . . *a lot* of little flame icons.

ELEVEN

Marco is still abnormally quiet when Sam meets him at the bike rack. Today, the shoe is on the other foot. *Sam* is usually the gloomy moodster, and Marco is the one to tease him out of it. But Sam doesn't really know how to get the banter started, and his own mood is a little suckier than usual. It doesn't help that the darkening sky is making it feel later than it is. There's still a strange orange tinge to the light, which reminds Sam of the filters directors use in movie scenes when bad things are about to happen . . . or when the world is ending.

Though he's been told countless times to never look directly at the sun, Sam's curiosity gets the best of him and he does. It's shockingly dim—and weirdly red orange. It's like he's looking at it with super-dark sunglasses on. Marco looks, too, and they both stand there staring for several seconds.

Neither says a word as they climb on their bikes.

The ride to the grove is easy—it's at about the same elevation as their houses and school, up above the village—so there aren't too many punishing hills. The boys ride in silence, keeping a slower-than-usual pace. Neither mentions the smoky air. There is no competition or egging on happening today. When they get to the trailhead, which is as far as they can go on their bikes, they lean them against the massive redwood that always greets them.

"Hey, big dude." Marco speaks at last, giving the tree's shaggy bark a pat.

The forest floor is soft with dropped needles and small branches, making the boys' footfalls almost silent, punctuated occasionally by the sound of a snapping twig. Just a hundred or so yards into the woods, they stop in the center of a circle. They're surrounded by a ring of five tall redwoods that almost command them to look up.

Sam traces the trunks with his eyes, following them up and up and up into the green canopy and the circle of dim sky in the center. He remembers his dad explaining that the five trees are actually one, growing out of the stump of a massive, ancient redwood that once stood in the middle and had probably been struck by lightning. These types of tree circles are a regular occurrence—a redwood survival tactic. Sam's mom calls them fairy rings.

Sweat trickles down Sam's back—it's as hot as it was yesterday and the smoke somehow makes it feel hotter. Still, the shifting light and shadows make him shiver. Marco mops his forehead with the corner of his T-shirt.

Sam wonders if working on the project today was such a good idea after all. But here they are. They might as well do the thing. He reaches for the camera case in his backpack as a memory threads its way through his body . . . the first time he came here . . .

He was with his dad on that visit, and his dad had been taking photos, of course. Sam was almost never the subject of his father's photos, because "you can't sit still for a second," but that day he was. He remembers how excited he'd felt when his dad told him where they were going. He was going to have a whole afternoon with just his dad! His mom had even packed them a picnic.

When they arrived at the grove midafternoon—too early for the shot—they had to wait for the sun to reach just the right angle. Sam wanted to explore the forest while they waited—the trees were huge! He spotted a monarch butterfly and wanted to chase it, to get a closer look at the orange-and-black wings, to see where it was going! But his father called him back immediately. "Sit," he told him. "Can't you just stay put? I don't have time to run after you right now!" So Sam sat.

After a long while, his dad said they were ready to take the picture. Sam didn't know what had changed, what made them "ready" now when they weren't before, but felt relieved that at last it was picture-taking time. He could finally do something!

That was before he understood that actually *taking* the picture took a long time as well. And that it *also* required a lot of keeping still.

Click click click. Click click click. "Sit on your knees," his dad instructed. "Lift your chin. No, not like that. Higher. A little lower. Keep your arms back . . ."

No matter what he did, Sam couldn't seem to get it right.

"Not like that!" his dad said again and again.

Is there another *way to lift my chin?* six-year-old Sam wondered.

When he was in the right position at last, Sam focused on not moving anything but his eyes. He could do this! Then a bird with a bright red crown landed nearby. Sam hopped up, excited, and flung his hand into the air to point so his dad would see it, too. He didn't mean to knock his dad's camera!

"What are you *doing*?" his father shouted. "This is expensive equipment!"

Sam shrank back into his kneeling sitting position, staring as hard as he could at the ground. The bird flew off, forgotten.

"I should have known this would never work," his dad complained as he packed everything up. He pulled on Sam's arm, moving fast toward the car, their picnic left beneath one of the trees.

His father didn't speak to him on the ride home, or for the rest of the day.

Now, looking through the lens of his father's camera, Sam tries to frame the same shot. It's the same time of day at the same time of year. Still, the light is all wrong. The smoke makes everything murky, at times nearly blotting out the sun.

Sam lowers the camera and lets his head fall back. He feels dumb. What made him think he could get a good shot with all this smoke? "I should have known this would never work!" he half shouts in frustration.

Marco looks up, startled. His wide eyes rest on Sam's face.

With a jolt, Sam realizes he is literally repeating his father's words. "I'm sorry. I don't know what I'm doing," Sam says, and means it. He can't look at Marco. He doesn't know what he's trying to accomplish, or how to get his dad's equipment to do what he wants, or even how to . . . keep going.

"It's the smoke," Marco says flatly. "It's changing everything."

Sam nods. He wills himself to pull it together. "Let's just go to your house and play video games," he says. "I'll let you win."

Marco *loves* video games. Before the photo project, they spent as many afternoons as their parents would allow defeating villains and escaping monsters on Marco's TV screen. Today, though, the offer doesn't seem to register. Marco just stands there, leaning into one of the redwood trees. Sam isn't even sure which one of them is holding up the other.

"Dude, let's just go home," Marco says finally. "I have homework, anyway."

Sam blinks. He can't remember a time that his friend wanted to go home before he had to—or wanted to get started on homework. He swallows, his throat scratchy. Just like Marco says, the smoke is changing everything.

Sam watches Marco start to walk out the way they'd come in. He begins to follow, then pauses in the tree circle. A twig breaks nearby, and Sam's head whips around. There, in his line of sight between two giant trees, he spots a pair of deer—a mama and a fawn. The little one still has lingering spots on its caramel-colored coat. The two deer take tiptoe steps on their long, slender legs, moving away.

Sam raises his camera to his eye, but the motion startles the deer and they disappear farther into the trees before he can get the shot.

Sam lets out a defeated breath and lifts his eyes again to the circle of redwoods. These trees have been growing for years, *hundreds* of years. The oldest redwoods are over two thousand years old. *Just how long*, Sam wonders, *would it take a fire to burn them all to nothing?*

CHAPTER
TWELVE

The angry roar of the fire can be heard for miles. It has become an endlessly feeding monster, one that is propelled onward by three pillars: fuel, oxygen, and heat. The pillars hold strong.

As the fire burns to the top of Bull Canyon, its intense heat extends farther and farther ahead of the flames, like an ambassador clearing the path. The heat quickly evaporates what little moisture remains in the air and speeds the blaze's movement. At the top of the canyon the firestorm pauses, like a cat waiting to pounce. Then, carried on a gust of wind, it makes an enormous leap.

The blaze doesn't bother to travel to the base of the canyon and back up the other side. It bridges the distance in an instant, sending masses of sparks and flaming embers into the tops of the smaller trees that line the crest of the next ridge. At the same time, the flames spread outward on all sides, growing larger, and hotter. Growing more deadly.

CHAPTER
THIRTEEN

Sam wakes with Goodboy snoring at his feet instead of on his pillow. He had completely ignored the no-dog-on-the-bed rule at the bedtime get-go and expected GB to have his head right next to his. It must have been too hot in the night for the pup to inch his way up to the prime position. Sam isn't exactly sad about this, because GB's breath is *not* his best feature. And though Vivian splurged on the donut bed not six feet away on the floor, all three of them know that during the four nights a week she spends at the hospital, dog-and-boy sleeping arrangements are free game.

Sam rolls over and grabs his phone. (There's a rule about keeping that out of his bedroom, too, but . . .) He rereads the text that came in after eleven, after he should have been asleep:

Working extra hours—lots going on here!

Have a great day at school.

See you tonight <3

Goodboy stands and stretches on the bed, lifting one back leg at a time and giving each one a good shake. He looks ridiculous, and Sam sits up to pull him closer and bury his face in the soft, wrinkly skin around the dog's neck and breathe in the doggy smell (which is *way* better than his breath). Then Sam gives his own stretch and swings his legs out of bed. He has to motivate himself to get out of the house this morning. No mom to ask him if he's eaten breakfast, packed his homework, fed the dog . . .

"Maybe it rained last night and put the fire out, huh?" Sam tells GB as they walk down the hall. He is trying to think positively, the way his mom tells him to. It hasn't rained in forever, but just before it got dark last night, the sea breeze had blown in, and it looked almost clear at their house.

As soon as he opens the back door it's obvious that Sam's dream of rain was just that: a dream. The sky looks grubbier than it did yesterday, and he can still hear helicopter blades whirring in the distance if he really listens.

In the kitchen, Sam fills GB's bowl and then pours himself a bowl of cereal. "Kibble for everybody, but no milk for you." He sets the dog dish down and settles on the couch to eat, breaking another one of their house rules.

He turns on the TV and then half wishes he hadn't. The news is all about the fire. It doubled in size overnight and now has a name: the Falcon Creek Fire. Sam drops his spoon into his bowl and focuses on the TV. The fire chief appears on-screen to take questions from reporters. Sam can't stop staring as the chief explains that they are facing "extreme fire conditions" and goes on to list all the things Sam's class had written on the whiteboard: wind, drought, rugged terrain, high temperatures . . . it goes on and on.

"We're doing all we can, but the current conditions are making it extremely difficult to contain this blaze. As always, safety is our top concern—both for our firefighters and for the members of our community."

The news anchor comes back on-screen, summarizing what the chief said and adding additional information for viewers. "Due to the unpredictable nature of this fire, some areas are being asked to evacuate." A map appears on-screen showing the county broken up into six zones, with the zones being evacuated highlighted in red. Sam leans forward to scan it. The village of Santa Bonita is in Zone 1, which is still green. Cyprus Ridge, where he and Marco live and where their school is, is in Zone 3. That's also green. The area east of Santa Bonita, near the hospital, is Zone 4. That's shaded yellow, which means they are on evacuation alert. So is Bull Canyon. Sam gulps. Hillcrest, right next to it, Zone 2, is red. It's being evacuated now.

"Local officials are doing all they can to help people get out safely. They request that anyone not being asked to evacuate avoid the designated exit routes."

Sam hits a button on the remote and the TV goes black. In the quiet of the living room, he hears his own shallow breath. He forces himself to take a deeper breath and reminds himself that Zone 3 is green. *Green.*

The house feels even emptier than it did before he turned on the television, and Sam wishes for the ten billionth time that his mom didn't have to work weird hours. He knows that working nights pays more. He knows she likes her job, and that she's good at it. He knows how much she cares about people. Last night's double shift is probably because of the fire. All those asthma kids she worries about must be showing up in the emergency room in droves.

Homework packed, teeth brushed, and dog fed, Sam is too anxious to wait for Marco. GB seems to sense his anxiety, because he's hopping on his short front legs to try to lick Sam's hand. As Sam lifts his backpack over his shoulder, the pup lets out a whimper.

"Sorry, GB. I know you would love school, but they would not love you." He gives his dog a goodbye pat, locks the door, and starts pedaling toward the Nuñezes'.

Sam is about halfway there when he spots Marco pedaling toward *him.*

"Sorry I'm late," he says. "Everyone at my house is going crazy because my aunt and uncle are on evacuation alert and we were already worried about Gabriela, because she is supposed—"

"Dude!" Sam feels instantly awful. Now he understands where Marco's head was the day before. Sam has gone with the Nuñez family to visit Marco's cousins in the valley lots of times . . . for birthdays and pool parties and touch football games. He didn't even register that they are in a yellow zone! And Gabriela! How could he forget that she works for CAL FIRE? Last June he'd gone to her graduation party and heard all about her plan to take classes and work for CAL FIRE.

"I'm so sorry! I forgot!"

Marco shrugs.

"Is Gabriela, is she—?"

"She hasn't been called yet. But Uncle Ruben thinks it might happen any second. Aunt Luz can't stop crying."

Sam doesn't know what to say. The hairs on the back of his neck are standing on end. He can't imagine wanting to fight something as dangerous and erratic as fire. But when Gabi had told them about her plans, she'd been super excited.

"That's why you were so quiet yesterday, huh? Worried about Gabi?" Sam feels awful for not realizing sooner. Gabriela is practically a big sister to Marco . . . and even to Sam.

Marco doesn't answer the questions. "Wanna race?" he asks, letting just half his mouth curl into a smile. "Me neither," he answers before Sam can. "Let's just go."

———

The boys are still ten feet away from their locker bank when Elsie calls out to them loudly. Her normally unruly blond hair is sticking up in all directions. "My friend Lisa's school is closed— they're using it for an evacuation center!" she announces. Her green eyes are wide with exhilaration and worry. "Her mom made her go to school anyway, though—to help out. There is a bunch of volunteers sorting through all the donations people are dropping off."

"Why not close our school?" Marco asks, looking a little envious as he works his combo.

"So you can get out of class?" Sam says, thinking he's making a joke.

Marco shoots him a look he's never seen . . . a mixture of anger and hurt and worry. "Dude. I'm not kidding. If this were an evac center, my family could come here." His eyes flash again. "I don't know where they're going to go," he adds quietly.

"It's too hard to get here," Elsie replies. "The main road into Santa Bonita would be jammed, and they don't want to shelter people here because getting back out would be almost impossible if the fire came over Maybeck Ridge. Plus, they need to keep both roads open—in case *we* all need to evacuate."

An image flashes in Sam's head: summer traffic on Sunday nights, the cars snaking their way at a crawl in an effort to get out of the village. Santa Bonita is special because it's so secluded, tucked into its hilly cove, but it's also a bit cut off.

———————

Mr. Billings is running his hand over his beard before class even begins. Yesterday's lists have disappeared and today the words EMERGENCY PREPAREDNESS are written in all caps on the whiteboard.

"It's important in any emergency situation to rely on the facts, and to also prepare for the unknown. The fire is not heading toward

Santa Bonita, but I think you'll all feel better and be safer if you and your families have a plan for what to do in case of an emergency . . . any emergency. So let's go ahead and think of some worst-case scenarios and what you might want or need if you found yourselves facing them."

Sam bites the skin on his thumb. He isn't sure about Billings's theory. Imagining the worst is sometimes the *actual* worst—Sam would know, since he spends a fair amount of time doing just that. Preparing, though, might be different. He does like a plan. Sam starts jotting down his own notes while the rest of the class throws out general ideas for what to pack or prepare.

1. Repurpose the earthquake bag.

Sam is sure there's a duffel somewhere that his dad put together, in case an earthquake left them without power, plumbing, and food. Maybe in the utility closet. A lot of the same stuff might be useful if they have to evacuate for fire.

2. Check batteries and radio.

Those should be in the earthquake bag for sure, but probably haven't been used in, well, ever.

3. Repack supplies (check expirations).
4. Pack food, leash, and bowl for Goodboy.

After item four, Sam stops. *What else?* If they have to leave the house, what will they take? There are so many things that can't be replaced!

His dad's photos instantly spring to mind. Sam's heart starts to thump harder, so hard he looks at Marco to see if he can hear it. Marco, though, is focused on Mr. Billings.

In his head, Sam pictures the portfolios and archival boxes full of his father's original photos and negatives—none of them digital and all of them flammable. There are so, so many things that just thinking about them makes it hard to breathe. He forces the image from his mind and tries to pay attention to what's going on in class.

"I don't care what they tell us, my family isn't going anywhere," Maverick announces. "We'll stay and protect our stuff!"

"You're just worried about your boat and ATV," Elsie teases.

The class laughs, but Mr. Billings isn't amused. "People who ignore evacuation orders run risks not only for themselves but for the emergency workers who are called in to protect them."

Maverick goes quiet, slouching in his seat.

"Your emergency plans should include not just what to take but where you will go, who you will stay with . . ." Mr. Billings says. Sam thinks about his grandparents on his mom's side. They live in Chicago, a plane ride or four-day road trip away. His other grandparents are gone. There's Aunt Laura, but she lives in Oregon and they have their own forest fires to worry about. Plus, his mom can't miss work. They'd have to go somewhere nearby. It's impossible. As class wraps up, Sam adds one last thing to the list: BECOME FIREPROOF.

CHAPTER

FOURTEEN

Marco and Sam meet at the bike rack after school like always, but instead of heading to a photo shoot or to Inside Scoop, they just head home. Neither boy says anything about their plans, or lack of them, as they ride several blocks in the same direction.

The smoke has gotten worse and bits of seemingly weightless ash have begun falling from the sky, landing on their clothes and skin and hair. Sam tries not to breathe too heavily. He hasn't checked the air quality index, but he can tell it sucks.

"See you tomorrow . . . I hope," Marco says just before their routes split in two directions. Sam stops pedaling for a second while that sinks in. Of course he will see Marco tomorrow . . . won't he?

"See you . . ."

Sam turns down his own street. A helicopter flies in his direction, coming from the east and flying so low that Sam can feel waves of hot air press against his body. He steadies his bike as he rides. It feels weird to be without Marco at 3:35 in the afternoon—they're *always* together after school—but he definitely wants to get home. His mom will be leaving for work in a couple of hours, and he needs to go over the emergency plan with her ASAP.

Goodboy isn't at the front door when Sam pushes it open. When he steps into the kitchen he understands why. His mom is grating cheese to top the minestrone—Sam's favorite soup. She made it for dinner, and GB is waiting . . . hoping . . . for a few shreds to end up on the kitchen floor. Sam can see a thin line of glistening drool hanging from the right side of his dog's closed mouth. There is nothing GB loves more than cheese.

"You're home early," his mom greets. "Did Marco have plans?"

Sam crosses the kitchen to give GB some love (avoiding the slobber), then sits down at the table and watches his mom finish grating. He wonders if she's really not worried about the fire, or if she's just acting like it to keep *him* from worrying. He shakes his head, uncertain.

"Earth to Sam," his mom says. "No Marco?"

"Oh, sorry," Sam replies. "No, not today."

Having given up on a cheesy snack, Goodboy rubs up against Sam's leg, vying for his other favorite thing: love. Sam strokes the pup's soft head, hedging, trying to think of a way to broach the emergency kit without freaking out his mom. Finally, he opens his mouth.

"We were talking about the Falcon Creek Fire at school today," he says slowly. "Mr. Billings told us all about emergency preparedness." He can't seem to look at his mom while he tells her about the class discussion. It's become a thing for him lately—not looking anyone in the eye when he's talking about something hard. "He says we all need to have emergency plans in place. That it's our responsibility."

His mom puts the hunk of ungrated cheese back in the refrigerator and returns to the stove, giving the soup a silent stir. Finally, she turns in his direction.

"An emergency plan is a good idea," she agrees, her words coming out slowly.

The words are barely out of her mouth when Sam is on his feet. He can sense there's something else she wants to say and doubts he wants to hear it. "Great!" he says, walking down the hall to get the earthquake kit. He drags the old yellow duffel out of the utility closet and into the kitchen, then begins to pull everything out, arranging the items in little piles. He can feel his mom watching him—feel her worrying about him. They both know that whenever something bothers Sam, he tries to do whatever he can to control it. He makes lists. He takes actions and checks off each item. He paces. He double-checks. He's always been like this—an overthinker. A worrier. And since his dad died? Well, let's just say that losing a parent didn't make him worry *less*.

"Can you hand me a piece of paper from the drawer?" Sam asks, still sitting on the floor. "And a pen?"

His mom lets out the tiniest of sighs and brings both to her son. She watches him start a new list, cross-checking the items and investigating the supplies.

"These granola bars are expired, the mini pry bar is missing, and some of the batteries are dead," Sam says, making notes. He flicks on the flashlight. "At least this thing is working!" He shines the light onto Goodboy, who leaps to his feet, thinking it's playtime.

Sam reaches out a petting hand. "Sorry, boy. We're just checking. I have to sort this stuff out."

Sam's mom is still watching, her face a cloud. Sam pretends not to notice.

"Honey, I think maybe you're overreacting a little bit," she says at last.

Sam pauses to look at her—just for half a second—a pair of dead batteries in his hand. Then he looks at the floor. "Mom, I think you're underreacting. A lot."

His mom goes quiet, and her eyes glisten. She looks at Sam surrounded by emergency gear, and bites her lower lip. After a moment she walks to the pantry, returning with a bag of trail mix. "To replace the granola bars."

Sam takes the bag and stuffs it into the duffel before hopping to his feet and giving Goodboy a pat. "Okay, let's get your things," he tells the pup, "then I can load up dad's photo boxes."

"Sammy, we don't need . . ." His mom squints in his direction, about to object, then trails off. She clears her throat to start over. "I know you want to save everything, but we have to be strategic. Dad's photos aren't essential."

Sam feels himself freeze in place. His heart begins to thud, his cheeks flush. He's a rapidly heating oven. How can she not understand this? How can she say that?

"They are totally essential!" Sam's voice is loud, tense. "His life is in those boxes! *We're* in those boxes. It's all that's left of him."

Sam's mom tries to step closer to him, but he pushes past and storms out of the kitchen. "You don't understand anything!" he shouts.

Furious, Sam keeps packing, throwing more stuff into a pile: Goodboy's leash and food, water, a new first aid kit. He strides into the den and starts going through his dad's photos, planning to combine the myriad prints into a handful of boxes. As he works, his breath begins to slow a bit, his body cools. Still, he is angry.

His mom knocks on the door to the den to say goodbye before she leaves for work. "I'll see you in the morning?" she says, making it sound like a question. "Call the Nuñezes if you need anything."

Sam doesn't acknowledge her—he just keeps sorting photos into piles. She lingers for a few seconds, then leaves, closing the door softly behind her. A moment later Sam hears the car start in the driveway.

"Bye!" he snarls sarcastically. Goodboy's ears go flat.

FIFTEEN

Sam groans in frustration as he opens yet another box of his dad's prints. He is surrounded by an arc of piles, several of which are already teetering from being stacked too high. He shifts his aching legs, careful not to knock them over.

What made you think you could condense his life's work into a handful of boxes? he asks himself chidingly. Choosing which prints to pack seems impossible. Honestly, it's impossible to consider leaving *any* of them behind.

Sam glances at the already-packed boxes of negative sleeves. For a moment he thinks about just taking those and leaving the prints. Then he shakes his head hard. *No.* Every single one of the completed images was developed and printed by his father. He held the paper in his hands, watched the images come to life in the chemical baths. He chose when to move each one from the developer to the stop bath.

Sam picks up an old photo of a wooded sunset—sequoias this time—gazing at the pale yellow wash of morning light showing through the dark green branches of the tree. His father had this way of capturing things so that it felt like he'd stopped time . . . Will Sam ever show the same skill? Does he want to?

The door to the den swings open and Goodboy saunters in, fresh from a stop at his water bowl. "Hey, boy," Sam greets him, not looking up. He sets the sequoia print on the tallest pile and is reaching for another when Goodboy plows through the circle, dripping water. His tail thwacks into a second pile, sending the prints flying out in all directions.

"Goodboy, no!" Sam shouts, covering his face with his hands in an effort not to explode. It almost works . . .

"We shoulda called you Badboy!" he shouts.

Goodboy's tail instantly tucks between his legs. With the tiniest of whimpers, he slinks off behind an easy chair. Sam sighs and wipes the droplets of water away, noticing that they only landed on the very edge of the print. Emotions clash inside him, roiling like unsettled ocean waves. He wants the fire to disappear. He wants his mom to be home. He wants his dad back!

He shoves aside a stack of "leave" photos and gets to his feet. A moment later he is lying on the floor next to the window, his head on Goodboy's torso, stroking the pit's soft flank.

GB is the best thing Sam has going at the moment, and none of this is his dog's fault. "You're a good boy, Goodboy," he says with a half smile. "I'm sorry I yelled at you." Goodboy whacks his tail on the carpeted floor, making soft thumps. Sam's breathing eases for the first time in hours. He doesn't want to be a yeller. Yelling is what his dad did. *And slinking off is what you used to do*, he adds to himself. A sliver of a thought snakes its way into his brain . . . a question. Does he really want his dad back?

The question is too scary to dwell on, but luckily, GB is right there. He raises his big square head and starts licking Sam's face. He covers every inch with just a few sloppy swipes. Clearly, all is forgiven.

"I love you, too, boy," Sam says, wiping his face with his shirt. Dog kisses are the best, but excess slobber can be a little much. The two stay there, reclined on the floor for several quiet moments. Sam can feel GB's heartbeat through his cheek. Finally the weight of Sam's ten-plus-pound head gets to be too much, and GB squirms to get up, kicking aside the curtains.

Sam sits up, too, and stares. The hazy, miscolored sunset sky looms just outside, casting the world in a surreal orange. The sun is so big behind the stripy haze it looks like a carnival balloon. Sam can't look. And he can't turn away. It feels like everything is coming apart . . .

The next thing Sam knows, he is on his feet and heading into the kitchen, an idea Goodboy clearly likes since he lumbers ahead. He hasn't been fed! Sam checks his watch . . . it's after seven. "Dinner's a little late again," he apologizes. He drops some kibble into the pup's bowl and makes toast while the soup heats on the stove. He is spooning up the last bite when his phone rings. Marco.

"Have you looked outside lately?" Marco asks without saying hello. "Sooooooo creepy. It's like we're on Mars or something."

Sam gives a half-hearted snort.

"Or maybe it's Venus. Isn't that the big red one that looks like it's burning?"

Sam knows Marco is trying to cheer him up, but it's not working.

The silence between the two boys hums across the telephone line. "Dude, it's going to be all right," Marco says. "Like Mr. Billings says, there are trained professionals fighting this fire. Gabi, for instance. You know how intense her training was. They know what they're doing."

Sam is still quiet. Marco doesn't wait to fill him in on everything he knows. "I wanted to tell you we just heard from her. Gabi. She says the fire is moving into the Los Madres National Forest, away from towns and people. A couple of the evacuation orders have even been lifted! It's going to be okay, Sam. Really."

"Really?"

"Dude, would I lie to you? No, nunca. Gabi got called in, but she's just glad there's something she can do, and she can focus now, since my aunt and uncle don't have to evacuate."

"That's so great," Sam agrees. "I'm glad you told me." He feels his shoulders relax, the soup in his stomach settle. This is the best news Sam has heard in days—maybe since he first smelled smoke in the village.

"Oh dang, my mom is calling me," Marco says. "Gotta go."

The boys click off and Sam does a quick kitchen cleanup while GB scours the floor for wayward crumbs. As he's putting the leftover soup into a container, Sam remembers yelling at his mom and feels a crashing wave of guilt. He hates fighting with her. He sighs and closes the refrigerator door. Yeah, he definitely overreacted. As soon as he finishes going through the prints, he'll text her and say he hopes her night is going well. Maybe he'll apologize, too.

In the den, Sam uses his gut to make the hard taking-or-leaving decisions, and creates totally new piles. All the prints are important, but not all the prints can come. He picks a few he knows his mother loves, a few he loves, and a few he *thinks*—he can't really be sure—his dad would want them to keep. It's the best he can do.

When all the prints are organized, he takes a hot shower and heads to bed, patting the pillow beside him for Goodboy, who hops up in a hurry. As far as Sam is concerned, GB can cover his whole half of the pillow in drool.

CHAPTER

SIXTEEN

Firefighters toil endlessly, day and night, battling the blaze. The fight is overwhelming and the efforts appear futile, like hummingbirds battling a dragon. The usual coastal humidity—swaths of dampness and fog that can keep wildfires this close to the Pacific from getting out of control—is doing nothing to thwart the ever-growing inferno. Still, the trained professionals do all they can. On the ground they clear three-foot-wide control lines around approachable areas of fire in hopes of containing the blaze. From above, helicopters dump water and bright pink flame retardant to try to slow the burn.

Marco isn't wrong. The fire *is* lurching away from populated towns, from people. The crews have so far been able to save structures by focusing their efforts. Evacuations *have* been lifted. And yet, mile-long stretches of pine, cypress, oaks, and redwood are going up in flames. A helicopter pilot looks down on smears of orange and red that stretch across seemingly endless terrain. The fire sends up thick plumes of smoke that rise skyward before fanning out like heavy coastal fog.

It is not fog.

In the vortex of the fire, sap sizzles and pops, louder than a jet engine. Some trees crash mightily to the forest floor, devoured to their cores, while others are left to stand like blackened skeletons, the fire moving on too quickly to complete its destruction.

The doe and her fawn stay clear of the flames, seeking refuge in open areas, creek beds, or ravines. Deer, foxes, bears, bobcats, mountain lions, and all kinds of smaller woodland creatures gather in clearings, ignoring their usual hunter-and-prey instincts. Their only goal is to survive.

So far, the doe has led them to enough clear water, enough grass and leaves, to sustain herself and her fawn. But it is getting harder. The smoke is thick, the heat oppressive. Their noses burn and their vision is blurred. The doe nuzzles her baby toward the edge of an unburned meadow, hoping to find a place to rest.

At three a.m. the wind shifts and begins to gust, forcing the fire in a different direction and speeding its growth. The fire roars up an unburned ridge and drops into a new valley . . . one that has never been burned, one that is loaded with fuel.

One that is a step closer to Santa Bonita.

SEVENTEEN

BZZZZZT BZZZZT. Sam wakes to his phone vibrating its way off his nightstand and catches it before it hits the floor. The time reads 5:07 a.m. There's a long string of notifications on the home screen. His eyes open wider as panic fills his chest. Goodboy raises his head off his drenched half of the pillow, looking a little worried himself. How long has his phone been ringing? Sam pushes the green button to answer.

"Hello?" he half shouts into the phone. There is nobody there. The call dropped. He checks the number. It was from his mom's cell, and she called repeatedly . . . five times in a row.

Take it easy, Sam tells himself, trying to swallow the panic that has now risen into his throat. *When you hear hoofbeats, think horses, not zebras,* he tells himself, repeating one of the phrases his mom likes to use to keep him from jumping instantly to the worst-case scenario. Problem is, his mom *never* calls during the night—she always texts so she won't wake him up. She leaves messages for him to get in the morning, usually letting him know she's not going to be there. Or maybe telling him to pull something out of the freezer to thaw for dinner.

Sam instinctively reaches a hand out for Goodboy, who is way better than a horse *or* a zebra, stroking his soft ear. GB's tail thumps on the bed. Sam's mom probably just had to stay longer at the hospital. She has to do that at least once a week—though she usually makes a point of not working over two shifts in a row. There must be a lot of extra work at the hospital because of the fire.

Goodboy's tail stills. He grunts and hunkers farther under the covers while Sam sits up and tries to call his mom back. The first call doesn't go through, and neither does the second or the third. With a pang he remembers that he forgot to text her last night after his shower, which he'd meant to do. "Dude!" he scolds himself out loud and dials a fourth time. Nothing.

Using both thumbs, he types in the message he'd meant to send the night before.

Sorry I yelled. Sorry I didn't say goodbye.

The soup was yummy. I hope you had a good night <3

Several seconds later, Sam's phone chimes. The text bounced. It's marked UNDELIVERED in red.

A lump forms in Sam's stomach. There's no denying it now. Something is very wrong. The situation is 100 percent zebras. He throws off the covers and goes to the window. Pulling the string to lift the blinds all the way up, he draws in a sharp breath. Sure it's early—the sun is barely up—but it's still darker than it should be, and also not dark at all. The sky glows in the distance—but not where the sun is rising. This is the glow of flames. Above the fire-light, a wall of smoke rises black, black, black into the sky.

Even inside, Sam's eyes burn and the smell of smoke is strong. His chest feels tight. If he takes a deep breath, there's a small ache in his lungs.

Things have changed overnight.

Sam pats his leg, beckoning GB, who reluctantly leaves the bed so the two of them can pad down the hall together to the living room. He hits a button on the remote and the TV comes on, still set to the local news. He hasn't found out what's happening, how close the fire is, or even if he has school, before the front door flies open and the lump in his stomach lurches upward, threatening to come flying out of his mouth.

"Dude!" Marco stands in the doorway, looking paler and way more serious than usual. "Dude, wake up, we gotta go."

Sam blinks back at his friend. Sam may still be in his pajamas, but he's very obviously awake! "You almost scared me to death!" he says, grabbing his heart (which *is* pounding like a heart attack victim's).

Marco just stands there, momentarily looking a little frozen, like a deer in headlights.

"I mean, aren't you a little early?" Sam asks. "What's up?"

Marco coughs and takes a couple of steps into the living room. Behind him, Sam spots Mr. Nuñez standing outside in the yard. Their family minivan is parked in the driveway. This is not just a way-too-early school pickup. This is something else.

"What's going on?" he asks again.

GB, who is running around Marco's legs trying to get as much hair on him as possible and begging for his hello tussle, wants to know the same thing. Marco, though, is ignoring the pup.

"You gotta get your stuff—we have to go," Marco says in a louder-than-usual voice.

"What? I can't . . ." Concerns swirl inside Sam, a whole tornado of worries forming and picking up speed. "Are we being evacuated?" The tornado threatens to touch down. What about his mom? Their house?? Everything in it??? This is what he'd been preparing for, of course, but now . . .

"Not yet. There's an evacuation alert for the other side of town and they closed the school. Your mom called our house when she couldn't reach you. She said she has to stay at the hospital, but she wants you to come with us."

"You talked to her?" Sam feels suspicious, and oddly jealous. There is nothing he'd like to hear more than his mom's voice right now. Even if she's still mad at him for being a jerk last night. Even if she said the word *fine* five hundred times. Even if she told him to think positive. "I can't get through to her," he says, holding up his phone.

Marco nods. "Yeah, my dad's been monitoring the emergency dispatch on the radio. There are some cell towers that burned—including the one between here and Bull Canyon. Our moms talked just before the service went out. We can still get through to some places, but it depends on the cell server."

"Let's go, boys!" Mr. Nuñez calls loudly from outside.

Marco looks around the room and his eyes stop on the bags piled by the door. "Is that all of your emergency stuff?"

Sam nods. "Yeah." He feels hot and cold at the same time. "Let me just get dressed." He has prepared for this, but he isn't ready. At all.

Marco follows him down the hall and keeps talking while Sam changes into jeans and a T-shirt. "Gabi is still working at the command center, so she's been sending us updates. She thinks she might get sent to fight the fire soon. She says she's ready, but she's only ever done mop-up before, you know? Going in after a fire has passed to douse the hot spots so it doesn't start up again? But this time she might end up on the front lines."

It's hard for Sam to even track what Marco is saying.

Dressed, Sam pauses. Should he brush his teeth? He hasn't even eaten breakfast. He's only half listening but still registers the worry in Marco's voice. There's a waver in it that Sam almost never hears. In fact, he's only ever heard it once before—at sleepaway camp three years ago when Marco was super homesick.

"Dude?" Marco asks, seeing that Sam has sort of frozen in the middle of his room. "You ready?"

Sam sucks in air and gives a nod. He is as ready as he'll ever be.

Back in the kitchen, Sam snaps on Goodboy's leash and grabs a cereal bar from a box on the counter, thrusting the half-empty box at Marco, who nods.

"Good thinking."

Sam unzips his backpack. He pulls out his textbooks and a binder, leaving them on the counter, and carefully places his dad's camera in the bottom before repacking. After zipping it up, he shoulders the bag and picks up the handle of the suitcase of prints with his free hand.

He exhales loudly. "Ready."

"Finally," Marco says, his mouth half-full of cereal bar. He turns and leads the way to the front door, grabbing the large yellow duffel as well as the bag of GB's stuff. Sam follows, stopping in the doorway. Should he lock the door? Will he be coming back? When? What if his mom comes home without a key?

"We've got to get going!" Mr. Nuñez calls again, nudging Sam to get a move on. Then he eyes Sam's bags. "We can't fit all of that! We have to fit five people . . . and the dog . . . in the car. Essentials only."

Sam hears Mr. Nuñez's words but can't quite process them. One bag. Essentials. That's all he can take.

"This is emergency gear?" Marco asks, hoisting the duffel to shoulder height. Sam nods. "And that?" Marco points at the large case of prints. Sam turns to put it back in the house. He can't open his mouth to speak. He can't tell Marco that these are what he has left of his dad. He can't admit that they are nonessential.

When he closes the door again, Sam feels like he's been punched in the stomach. The air has gone out of him, and watching Mr. Nuñez toss their outdoor chairs off the porch makes him feel even more battered.

"What are you doing?" he asks. He looks down the driveway and sees the rest of their outdoor furniture and the tank from their outdoor grill have all been piled together, a hurried relocation. Is Mr. Nuñez trashing the place?

"What are you *doing*?" Sam asks again, a little heatedly.

"You want to get anything that can burn away from the house," Mr. Nuñez replies. "Especially that propane. As a precaution," he adds, apparently seeing the panic on Sam's face.

Sam can't even nod. He watches Marco load the yellow bag into the back of the sticker-covered minivan and waits while he stacks the bag of GB's stuff on top.

As Sam folds himself into one of the captain's chair seats in the middle row, he hides his backpack. That *is* essential . . . at least to Sam.

Questions bounce around in his head like a tipped-over bucket of rubber balls. How far away is the fire right now? Which way is it burning? Where the heck are they going? And maybe most important, how will his mom know where to find him?

Goodboy jumps in after Sam, settling at his feet. Marco rides in the front with his dad, and Sam is glad it's only him and GB in the back. He leans his head into the headrest and closes his burning, itchy eyes, picturing the suitcase sitting on the floor of the kitchen. Alone. Out of place. He can't look at anyone, anyway. He feels a little like he felt at his dad's memorial—numb.

"Buckle up," Mr. Nuñez says. He presses a button and the door next to Sam slides shut.

CHAPTER
EIGHTEEN

The drive to the Nuñez house is short, but it feels long because it's unusually quiet. A high school history teacher, Mr. Nuñez almost never misses an opportunity to monologue to any captive kid audience, pontificating in an effort to share *all* the knowledge he has about *everything* . . . a habit Sam usually finds comforting, not to mention informative!

Today, though, Mr. Nuñez, Sam, and Marco ride in silence. And Sam is glad.

He stares out the window, swallowing repeatedly, trying to soothe the ache in his throat and the bigger ache in his chest. The dim light is unnerving, and the headlights cut through only a few feet of the thick slurry of smoke and fog. The dotted lines down the center of the road appear two by two, and when they turn in to

Marco's driveway, Sam can barely make out the Nuñezes' porch with its uncarved pumpkins waiting patiently for Halloween.

Halloween. The thought of the sugar-and-costume-filled holiday jolts Sam. He had forgotten all about his favorite holiday! Sam has spent nearly every Halloween at Marco's house, and since his dad died, his mom has joined him. There's always chili loaded with guacamole and cheese, corn bread, cider, and a towering heap of homemade doughnuts. That has been his Halloween normal for as long as he can remember. As he walks up the front steps and passes the giant pumpkins, Sam wonders if things will ever be normal again.

"Sammy!" Sofia, Marco's six-year-old sister, wraps herself around Sam's legs as soon as he steps in the door. At least *she* seems normal.

"Hi, Sof." Sam manages a smile. The first grader worships him. He's like a second big brother who never gets annoyed. Well, almost never. When she doesn't let go of his legs, Sam nearly falls flat on his face in the entry. Luckily, Sofia spots Goodboy and releases Sam just in time to wrap herself around the dog instead.

"GBeeeeeeee!" she singsongs.

Sofia is even more obsessed with Goodboy than she is with Sam. The feeling is mutual. The lovefest between GB and Sofia is immediately on, and it takes up the entire front hall, blocking anyone from moving in or out the door.

Marco finally leaps over them both and heads with Sam to the living room. The two boys sit next to each other on the L-shaped couch. They automatically flop down in their usual game-playing seats—muscle memory taking over. But the controllers stay in the box below the TV. Marco's mom, Anita, is stationed at the other end of the sofa, drinking coffee out of a travel mug and watching the news.

"Did you have breakfast, mijo?" she asks Sam without taking her eyes from the TV. "Are you hungry?"

"No," Sam answers. His cereal bar sits untouched in his pocket. The last thing he wants to do right now is eat.

On the screen, the newscaster's expression is somber. "Firefighters had hoped that lower night temperatures might slow the blaze," he reports. "But those lower temperatures never materialized. Winds and unusually low humidity are constantly intensifying the Falcon Creek Fire, which continues to burn and has spawned several smaller fires in the area. As of six thirty a.m. this morning, the fire is less than fifteen percent contained."

Fifteen percent, Sam thinks as the screen switches to a map view. That's not even close to a quarter. If there is *any* good news, it's that the fire is burning the peaks opposite Cypress Ridge, where Sam and Marco live. They don't think it will jump Falcon Creek—actually more like a river than a creek—because the waterway forms a natural control line. The other good news is that no structures have burned. Yet.

The newscaster continues to drone on about defensible space, climate change, and the uptick in natural disasters. He talks about how the fire is really a *complex* . . . several dangerous fires burning at once. Sam's head feels as full of smoke as the air. He tries to ignore its throbbing. When the weather report comes on with cautions to stay indoors, Mrs. Nuñez moves closer to put a comforting arm around Marco.

Sam is suddenly on his feet. Most of the time he feels totally at home at the Nuñez house . . . Marco's mom even calls him mijo—her son—in Spanish. Today, though, everything feels wrong. He doesn't want to be here. He wants to be at home. He wants to be with his *own* mom.

"Are you okay?" Mrs. Nuñez asks. Sam just stands there, with nowhere to go. He can't return her gaze. He can only nod as he glances around for Goodboy. He needs Goodboy. But the pushover pup is probably in Sofia's bedroom getting dressed up in something humiliating, wagging his way through it like the awesome dog he is. The thought almost gets the corners of Sam's mouth to curve into a smile. Almost.

Sam can feel Mrs. Nuñez's eyes on him now, so he sits back down in the easy chair opposite the sofa. Mr. Nuñez comes in from the kitchen with his own cup of coffee, taking his place on the couch between his wife and son.

"Have you heard anything new from Gabriela?" Mrs. Nuñez asks.

Mr. Nuñez's Adam's apple bobs before his head. He doesn't really want to answer. "Sí. She's been dispatched."

Anita Nuñez bites both her lips, making them almost disappear between her teeth. She closes her eyes in what Sam imagines is a silent prayer for her niece. When they open, she starts speaking rapid-fire Spanish to her husband. Although Sam knows some Spanish from his years with the Nuñez family, he can't follow their quick conversation. He's not sure he wants to.

"Goodboy!" he calls, patting his leg. "GB!" He is on his feet again, suddenly desperate for his dog. Goodboy is literally half of Sam's family. He needs him. Now.

Sam walks toward the bedroom Marco and Sofia share, fully expecting to see the pit's broad head decked out in a stupid hat or bow or worse. (Sofia once made him wear a cereal box Minecraft helmet.) Instead, he finds Sofia lying on the carpet with her sneakered feet in the air. Alone.

"Where's GB?" Sam asks.

"Oh, he was scratching at the back door, so I let him out," Sofia answers. Sam blinks as this sinks in, then he bolts for the back door. There's no fence around the Nuñezes' forested property!

"GB!" Sam shouts before he's even outside. "GB!" he shouts again from the back porch. He whistles and waits, then squeezes his eyes shut, picturing Goodboy trotting out of the smoky gloom with a big, slobbery dog grin on his face.

When Sam opens his eyes, his dog is not there.

CHAPTER
NINETEEN

Goodboy!"

"Here, Goodboy!"

"Goodboy, come!"

"GB!"

As soon as they hear Sam calling, the entire Nuñez family joins in the search for GB. Four voices shout into the smoky woods behind the house, each of them ignoring their scratchy, aching throats. The family doesn't have any neighbors behind their home, so they've never felt the need to fence their yard . . . until right this second.

"I'm sorry." Sofia sniffles. She slides her hand into Sam's. "I didn't think he'd run off."

Sam doesn't want to be mad, and he feels bad that Sofia is crying.

But he can't seem to keep the waves of anger from crashing over his head. He drops her hand almost immediately.

There's no way Sof could have known GB would run off. Normally he sticks close. But with the fire, nothing seems normal. Nothing *is* normal, Sam reminds himself. It's making them all anxious. Even GB. Still, Sam wishes Sofia hadn't let his dog out. He wishes she had asked him first.

"Goodboy!" Sofia calls again, her voice hitching.

Sam turns away. His hands curl into fists and he stomps farther into the woods, out beyond the area that the family keeps cleared. He passes stands of trees. Bushes scratch at his arms, and his feet sink slightly into the forest floor, which is thick with fallen leaves and needles. Sam cups his hands around his mouth and shouts again.

"Gooodboooy!"

His voice is raspy. He looks back and can't see the Nuñez house. How far could GB have gotten? Where would he go?

As soon as Sam asks himself the question, he knows the answer. GB went to the same place Sam wants to go. Goodboy went home.

Sam feels his chest constrict. *Home!*

Standing still, he can hear the Nuñezes calling for his dog on the other sides of the house. He hears another noise, too . . . an unfamiliar one. It's not a ringtone, or a timer. It sounds like a loud, buzzing alarm.

Sam runs back, protecting his face from branches with his arm and dodging trees. He steps into the clearing to see Mr. Nuñez walking around the corner of the house. He somehow looks older than he did yesterday, or even a few hours ago. He has one hand on his head, his fingers tangled in his thick, salt-and-pepper hair. In his other hand he holds his cell phone. His eyes are locked on the screen.

"This is it," Mr. Nuñez announces loudly. "They're evacuating zone three. That's us. We have to go."

Sam freezes. "I can't go without Goodboy!" He hesitates before adding, "I'm sure he went back to our house. I have to get him." Sam hates the whine he can hear in his own voice, but he's desperate. And frozen. He stares at the ground and hears footsteps coming closer.

A heavy hand lands on his rigid shoulder. Mr. Nuñez is still reading from his phone screen. "Sam, they're closing the road going south. All traffic is being directed north and east—away from town. We can't go back to your house."

It is all Sam can do to keep breathing.

"Goodboy is smart. He'll run *away* from the fire if it comes. Your dog is going to be fine."

Sam sucks in air and feels the dull ache in his lungs. *Fine.* Goodboy will not be fine. Not without him. He knows this to his core but can't say it out loud.

"Are you sure GB will be okay?" Sofia asks. She reaches up to find her dad's free hand. Sam can see tear tracks on her face.

"He'll be fine," Mr. Nuñez reassures her.

That word again.

"Let's load up!" Mr. Nuñez is all business. He sounds like a teacher again, calling the kids back from recess.

Sam is not reassured. "Please," he says, finally finding his voice. "Can't we wait a few more minutes? He might come back!" Sam begs, though he knows Goodboy isn't coming back. Not back here, anyway.

"I'm sorry." Mr. Nuñez turns and walks toward the house, herding Sofia in front of him. He calls to Marco and Mrs. Nuñez in Spanish, probably telling them to hurry to get their things from inside. Sam follows them in, feeling like an outsider—a feeling he's never had with this family before today.

Being in the house feels awful. Sam quickly grabs his backpack and walks out to the driveway. He tries to shake off the sense of not belonging—the Nuñez family is trying to help—but it sticks to him as tightly as a barnacle on an ocean rock. His whole body has that needle-pricking feeling, like when his arm or leg falls asleep. He can't even make himself open the car door.

"Everyone in the car in five minutes!" he hears Mr. Nuñez yell from inside. Sam stands stock-still. He feels angry. So angry! Then sad. Then angry again. And most of all, helpless.

His vision gets wavy as tears threaten. Then his eyes lock on something leaning against the porch rail. Something familiar, something orange. Marco's bike.

It's time to FLY.

CHAPTER

TWENTY

S am puts on his backpack and runs toward the bike. He doesn't have much time. Any second now, everyone will be coming out to get in the car, to evacuate, and he's got to be out of here. He can't evacuate. Not yet, and not without GB.

When he reaches the Huffy he throws his leg over the bar. He plants his feet on the pedals, pushes off, and starts pumping without sitting down. He wants to get as much leverage and speed as he can . . . especially until he gets around the corner.

It's only eight a.m., but you'd never know it by the sky. The light is even weirder today. This is the time that Sam and Marco would usually be leaving for school. Instead, Sam is riding away from his best friend and the Nuñez family. Instead, he is breaking the law.

Sam glances over his shoulder to make sure he can't see Marco's house or car, and for the first time feels almost grateful for the smoke, which makes it hard to see anything clearly. As he takes the turn onto Joaquin Gully—the main road that bisects the subdivisions in Cypress Ridge—he thinks he hears someone call his name but can't be sure. Not that it matters . . . he's not stopping. He pedals a little harder, whizzing down the larger road that will pass the turnoff to his house before winding down to a fork that leads to school in one direction and town in the other.

He hasn't gone far when he sees headlights coming toward him and pulls onto the shoulder, away from the oncoming traffic. There are no lights on FLY, just reflectors. A boy on a bike in the smoke might be hard to see, and easy to hit!

A large pickup truck passes, heading east. Then an SUV and a sedan, followed by a motorcycle and another SUV. Within minutes, there are cars and cars and cars, all slowly snaking their way along the road. Everyone is evacuating. Everyone had been ready and waiting for this moment.

Someone honks as they drive past Sam, but they don't stop. A few moments later, Sam turns his head in time to recognize a kid from humanities class, Sarah Jennings, in the back seat of a silver Subaru. Luckily, she doesn't look his way.

Sam stands to crank up a hill when a big white truck slows down. The driver leans out and yells, "You're going the wrong way!"

Sam turns away, hoping the guy didn't see his face, hoping he'll just keep going. If Sam is recognized, it won't be long until everyone in Santa Bonita knows he's disobeying the evacuation order.

News spreads in the village faster than warm butter on hot toast—he has to get off Joaquin Gully now, before his regular turnoff.

FLY is definitely not a mountain bike, but Sam knows there's a single-track trail ahead that will keep him off the main evacuation route and that *also* offers a pretty direct path to his house. When he spots the trailhead he veers off and takes it, hoping the Huffy's tires hold up and the chain stays on.

The ride is jarring to say the least. Sam's teeth knock as he bumps along the trail, but he tells himself over and over that it's worth it. This is probably the route that GB took, anyway—he knows it because it's the way they walk to Marco's sometimes. After three turns, Sam can make out the back of a house through the trees—Hank's place. Even with burning, watery eyes he can see Hank's Chevy in the driveway. The truck is probably as old as Hank, but he prides himself on keeping it running, especially since it doesn't have anything newfangled like a microchip that tells the engine what to do. Hank prides himself on being extremely low-tech in general. He calls himself a Luddite and is totally opposed to anything computerized. "If I can't fix it myself, I probably don't need it," he likes to say, always adding, "the only chips I like go great with salsa and guacamole."

Sam screws up his mouth and hits the brakes. Without a cell phone, Hank might not even know about the evacuation order. Glancing quickly over his shoulder, he rolls FLY back out onto the street and pedals toward Hank's house. It'll only take a second to let him know he's got to go.

As he pedals, a new thought occurs to Sam: Hank might have a landline that he can use to call his mom, or at least the hospital!

Dropping the Huffy in the dust by Hank's truck, Sam takes the front stairs two at a time. He knocks on the door, softly at first, then harder when there's no answer. He's about to give up and jump back on FLY when the door opens.

"Sam?" Hank squints, blinking. "What are you doing here?" The creases in the old guy's face deepen, revealing his surprise.

"There's . . . an . . . evacuation . . ." Sam pants. "The fire." It's hard to catch his breath. Sam wonders if his heart is pounding from the ride or the adrenaline. "You have to evacuate!"

Hank's expression barely changes, then his eyebrows come down a few centimeters to rest like hairy white caterpillars above his squinty eyes. "Yeah, I don't do that," he says bluntly.

"You don't *evacuate*?" Sam asks. He's not sure what to say to that. He knows what Mr. Billings would say—that folks who don't follow evacuation orders create more problems for firefighters and take attention away from the flames—but he doesn't feel right saying something like that to someone so much older than he is. And of course he isn't exactly leaving either . . . yet.

As soon as Sam has his dog, he'll figure out how to get out of here, though. Then he'll make his way to his mom. He can't *wait* to evacuate! "Um, uh, okay," he finally stammers and then remembers to ask, "can I use your phone?"

Hank shakes his head slowly. "Well, you could, but the power's just gone out and the darn thing doesn't work without electricity."

Sam notices that the hallway behind Hank is dark. Like, *dark*, dark. "Oh . . . kay." Sam looks down at his feet, then up at the sky, where the rising sun looks like a giant, glowing basketball.

Don't panic, don't panic, don't panic, he tells himself. But the words don't help. *Stick to the plan. Get GB. Get to Mom*, he tells himself instead. One step at a time. That's all he has to do.

"Okay, thanks anyway!" Sam says, then turns and races back down the steps. "I think you should get out of here while you can!" he calls back over his shoulder as he pedals away. Hank raises a hand to wave but makes no reply.

Get GB. Get to Mom. Get GB. Get to Mom. Sam repeats his plan in rhythm with his pedaling. He takes the connector trail back to the road and then turns into his driveway.

"He's gotta be there," Sam says out loud as he peers toward the porch. He's sure GB is at home. And his mom might even be there by now, too! He lets the hope rise in him like a helium balloon.

Then he sees the furniture still scattered on the driveway. It looks like a bomb has gone off.

He sees the empty porch. No Goodboy.

He sees the empty driveway. No mom.

The Huffy rolls to a stop by the stair rail. Sam lets it drop on the asphalt, then sinks to his knees beside it. "Goodboy!" he calls, though he already knows it's no use. Goodboy is not here.

Sam is all alone.

CHAPTER

TWENTY-ONE

A s the shrouded sun moves upward in the sky, temperatures climb with it. The fire burns on, executing its own will, its own power, its own weather pattern.

Sweat rushes in streams down the limbs of the firefighters, who risk their lives to toil endlessly while the roaring blaze sends swirling vortexes of flames into the sky.

In the cockpit of a Grumman S-2T air tanker, a pilot prepares for takeoff, flipping switches and checking gauges. He operates the controls with the ease of someone who has been doing this for decades, because he has. He's been fighting fires for thirty years. Airborne, the pilot can see the growing fire as he approaches. He tries to get over it, to drop the eight hundred gallons of water in his tanks on the target, but the fire's scorching updrafts grab ahold of the plane, tossing it back and forth like a ball thrown between a pair of bullies playing keep-away. Cursing under his breath, the pilot struggles to steer the plane safely back out of the firestorm. It takes longer than usual. Beads of sweat gather on his brow. When he's finally free of the buffeting winds, he mops his face and grabs the radio.

"Can't get in," he reports, his voice shaking with fatigue and relief. "Too many updrafts. Too dangerous."

The radio is silent for a full minute. "Head to Santa Bonita," the commander finally instructs. "Drop on any buildings that might be at risk." He hesitates, then adds, "There should be plenty."

"Copy," the pilot replies. He steers the plane to the quaint coastal town that lies in the valley between the rugged shore and the rising mountain range. He's familiar with the spot—he and his family vacation here every summer.

On the ground, several miles from the flames, Gabriela works alongside a team of firefighters. She and six others work in a line with special tools that are part rake and part shovel. They dig and scratch down to the bare earth, clearing away debris and grass. Ahead of them, half a dozen more firefighters work with axes and chain saws to remove dead branches, brush, and small trees. Each firefighter moving along the line behind those in front, improving the boundary until they've created a three-foot-wide barrier, devoid of fuel.

Gabi lets out a strangled cough. Her body aches with fatigue; her lungs burn from inhaling smoke despite her fire suit and helmet.

Her earplugs do little to keep the roar of the chain saws from screaming in her ears. She and her team have been working for three hours. She doesn't know how long their shift will run. The boundary they've created is a quarter mile from Falcon Creek. They are hoping that the line will be enough to stop the fire, or at least slow it down so that it won't be able to cross the nearly twenty-foot width of Falcon Creek.

Gabi thrusts her tool into the trench again and again, ignoring the heat. A few feet away, a firefighter she can't identify through their gear drops to their knees. A medic comes to evaluate, and the fighter is pulled from the line. No one replaces them.

Gabi keeps working. She thinks of her family. She thinks of her home. She has trained for this. She wanted this. This is her job.

Finally, a whistle blows. They've done all they can here . . . or perhaps a fresh crew has arrived to replace them.

"Let's go, let's go!" one of the chiefs calls. Gabi squints into the distance. She can see flames licking the trees. She guesses the fire front is within a mile of them now. She picks up her tool and the one left by the departed firefighter. She hauls them back to the truck and piles into the back, along with several other crew members. As they rumble over the rough terrain, Gabi looks back, thinking that the trench looks ridiculously narrow. She prays that the line holds.

TWENTY-TWO

Crouched in the driveway, Sam has no choice but to let the tears fall. It was so stupid to come here—he knows that now. He wipes his eyes with his dirty sleeve and feels grit smearing across his face. He doesn't care. His dad is dead. There is a wildfire taking over his town. He can't find his mom or dog . . . his family . . .

A fresh batch of tears springs to Sam's eyes and begin to roll down his cheeks. He drops his head into his hands and his butt to the ground. He has to get out of here—he knows that. The smoke is heavier than ever, the sky an ominous orange gray. The evacuation order has been issued. But he can't seem to move. He car only sit here and cry.

Sam is still sitting in his driveway when something wet and

warm noses his ear. He raises his head and looks into the sweetest brown eyes in the world.

"GB!" he shouts and throws his arms around his dog's neck.

"Good boy, Goodboy!" Sam chokes out while the pup licks every centimeter of his face, kissing away his tears and maybe even cleaning a bit of the soot. Sam buries his nose in Goodboy's fur, feeling a happy tingle of relief flow through him. Together, they roll off the drive and onto the dry lawn, tussling, teasing . . . just happy to be together. The grass prickles, but Sam can't remember the last time something felt so good. He presses his cheek against the soft fur on Goodboy's wide head and inhales deeply. He is instantly choked by the thickening smoke.

The resulting coughing fit brings him back to his senses.

Sam sits up. The situation hasn't changed—he just has his dog back. The danger is still real. He has to figure out what to do, and fast. *Think!* He tells himself.

Sam gets to his feet and leads Goodboy into the house and, realizing he *really* has to pee, uses the bathroom. He flips a light switch—it's dark indoors thanks to the smoke—before remembering the power is out.

Is it smokier than it was this morning? he wonders. It's definitely darker. In the kitchen, Sam smells a hint of his mom's favorite cinnamon tea through the fire fumes, and his chest constricts with worry. He checks his phone—no phone or text messages—and tries to make a call, knowing it won't go through.

All he wants, now that he has GB, is to stop fleeing and

panicking and wait for his mom to come back. She'll be here right after work, right? She'll come home. That's what she does every day.

Every normal day, Sam corrects himself.

He hadn't wanted to leave this morning—he wanted to wait for his mom. And after that, at the Nuñezes', he just wanted to feel at home. And here he is, back in his own home, and it feels just as wrong as being at his friend's house did. Was coming back here all for nothing?

A pang of guilt layers onto Sam's worry as he considers his friend's family. The Nuñezes are probably in a panic because he just took off. Even if they figure out where he's gone, they can't come get him. As if to punctuate that thought, a helicopter thunders overhead, crazy close to the ground. So close it rattles the windows.

"We gotta get out of here," Sam tells GB. He needs to stick to the plan. He has GB. Now he needs to get to his mom. "We're going to the hospital."

With a gulp, Sam realizes that everything except his backpack is in the back of the Nuñezes' car. He has none of his carefully packed emergency gear, no food for Goodboy. Not even his phone charger (not that it would do any good without electricity!).

"I'm giving myself two minutes to get some important stuff together," he tells GB, whose ears prick in response. The pup follows him to the bathroom, a hall closet, the kitchen . . . Sam shoves some crackers, a couple of apples, and GB's favorite dog treats into the bag. He grabs the backup leash. At the last second, he grabs an extra water bottle. Finally, the twosome head outside.

With GB on the leash, Sam throws a leg over the bar of the Huffy and pushes off. Right away the bike feels weird.

"What the . . ." Sam looks down. The problem is easy to see. FLY's front tire is completely flat. The Huffy will not be taking off again anytime soon. "Dang it!"

The bike is useless. Frustrated, Sam tosses it aside and heads down the driveway on foot, with Goodboy trotting alongside him.

Don't panic, don't panic, don't panic, he tells himself, even as he feels the panic rising from the pit of his stomach into his chest. He makes the mistake of inhaling deeply again. Instead of oxygen flowing into his lungs and calming him down, polluted air rushes in to strangle him and spurs another coughing fit. When it finally subsides, Sam is left wheezing and his throat feels like it's lined with fish scales pushed in the wrong direction. He leans over to put his hands on his knees until he half catches his breath. Goodboy waits patiently, tail gently wagging, clearly unsure how to comfort his boy.

Feeling a little woozy and no closer to figuring a better solution, Sam lifts his head. He can see something approaching . . . an unidentifiable shape. "What the . . ." He squints, trying to make out the form. He has no idea what is coming toward them.

"Woof!" Goodboy barks. "Woof, woof!" The dog takes off at a hard run, yanking the leash and pulling Sam to the ground.

TWENTY-THREE

O*ooof!* Sam tumbles forward, landing hard and letting go of the leash. Goodboy has nearly closed the gap between him and the thing coming toward them. Sam blinks at the figure, trying to focus. Whatever it is, it is flailing like some kind of giant wayward chicken, and it also sort of . . . sparkles?!

The thing finally comes to a halt.

Goodboy continues barking, making a sound that Sam struggles to identify: Is it a greeting or an alarm?

Then "woof!" he barks again, and it's unmistakable. Goodboy is happy!

Sam's confusion is off the charts . . . until he's finally able to make out the pom-pommed handlebars of a sparkly purple bike.

Relieved and more than a little slaphappy, he cracks up and rises to his knees, chortling.

"Dude!" is all he can say. It's Marco on his little sister's bike, which is so small his legs are bowing out like a chicken's, practically knocking into the tassled handlebars with every turn of the pedals. It's too much.

"No bowing necessary," Marco quips, nodding at Sam's kneeling position, and greeting GB. "Although I will be collecting a bike rental fee later."

Stepping awkwardly off the small purple bike, Marco helps Sam to his feet. Sam throws his arms around Marco's shoulders, squeezing tight. He has never been so happy to see his best friend.

"I love you, too, Sammy," Marco says, squeezing back and then patting Sam's back. "But let's get out of here. I don't want to die before my parents have a chance to kill me."

Marco scans the area, looking perplexed. "So, um . . . where's my bike?" he asks. "'Cause you're the one riding Purplicious on the way back . . ."

Sam shakes his head. "FLY's back there." He nods toward the porch. "With a flat tire," he adds glumly. "I had to take the mountain bike trail to my house because of all the traffic. Might have ridden over a sharp rock." Sam expects Marco to respond with a "We can add the repair to the rental fee," but his friend just looks as deflated as FLY's tire—like that last bit of news is the final straw. He bows his head in a tiny moment of silence, whether for FLY or their current situation isn't clear.

"We can probably fix it," Sam says, knowing that is not a viable option right now . . . even if they did have the right supplies.

"Not soon enough for us to get the heck out of here . . ." Marco trails off, thinking. Then his face brightens. "Hey, doesn't Maverick live near here?"

Sam nods and points to a big house on the corner, where his street meets Joaquin Gully. "Yeah. Right there."

"I can't believe I'm saying this, but let's hope he really does have a boat and a trailer and a brand-spanking-new ATV in that three-car garage of his."

It takes Sam a few seconds to understand what his friend is saying. "You want to steal Maverick's ATV?" His eyebrows practically merge with his hairline.

Marco nods and starts moving toward the large corner house without waiting to see if Sam is on board with this plan. "Unless you have a better idea?"

"Right." Sam follows. Hope and anxiety flow through his body in equal measure—at least they're doing *something*. Two minutes later, the boys and Goodboy are standing in front of Maverick's garage, staring at the electronic keypad that operates the door.

"Won't open without power," Sam says. They're stumped again!

Goodboy sits down, like he knows this might take awhile.

"Duuuude." Marco sounds only a little bit defeated. "Let's try the door to the house." He trots off in that direction. Sam sees him reach for the handle, but Marco's body blocks the action.

"Bingo!" Marco calls.

The front door is unlocked. Maverick or his parents must have listened to the emergency advice to leave homes open so firefighters can do whatever is needed to save people or structures. Marco holds open the heavy wooden door and all three of them step into the house.

Even with the curtains open, it's dark inside. Marco and Sam dig out their practically useless phones and use flashlight apps to guide them bumblingly to the kitchen and then the garage, which is darker still. They lift the tiny beams and shine them around the cavernous space. Sure enough, the three-stall building holds a boat, a trailer, and a Honda Rubicon.

"Thank you, Maverick!" Marco says softly as he makes a beeline for the four-wheeler. "The key is in the ignition!" he hoots. "No hot-wiring required!"

Sam is astounded. "You know how to *hot-wire*?" Marco is full of surprises.

Marco shrugs. "No. I was going to have you do that."

Still joking. Always joking. Sam provides the smallest of courtesy laughs and shines his light around the large space—they're not in the clear yet. They got into the garage—check. They found an ATV with key in the ignition—check. Only one component to this plan is missing . . . well, other than actually driving the thing . . .

"How are we going to get it out of here?" Marco asks, reading Sam's mind.

Sam knows for a fact that Marco has never driven an ATV but has ridden with his cousins plenty. He's praying that's enough to pull this craziness off. Still, there's no way Marco can start his driving career by ramming through a garage door. He's not an action hero; he's a future comedian.

Sam's mind stalks in circles, wrestling with this problem. He shines his light up at the ceiling and traces it along the automatic mechanism that raises and lowers the garage doors. He spots a red handle dangling from a short rope that attaches to the pulley system. There are three of them—one for each door.

"Manual release!" he half shouts. It makes total sense for a garage to have a manual system to open the doors in an emergency . . . at least that's what Sam tells himself as he positions himself beneath the toggle connected to the ATV's door. He has to jump to grab it, but he catches the handle dangling over the Rubicon and pulls as hard as he can. The scraping sound of metal wheels on a metal track echoes loudly in the garage as the big door begins to open. After one more hard pull, the door is open far enough for the ATV to pass through.

"Dude!" Marco cheers, hopping onto the Rubicon. "Let's go!"

Sam climbs onto the seat behind Marco and pats the narrow space between the two boys. Goodboy hesitates only slightly before leaping up and wedging his bottom down so he's sitting between them.

Marco turns the key and the engine revs. It's loud! "Hang on!" he shouts.

Half a second later, the four-wheeler roars out of Maverick's garage and lurches wildly down the driveway.

CHAPTER
TWENTY-FOUR

The fire roars over the top of a ridge, moving toward the coast. Several natural barriers stand between the flames and the village of Santa Bonita: valleys that might slow the approach when flames descend into them, out of reach of the gusting winds, and creeks that form natural lines—lines that are hard for the fire to cross. This is especially true of Falcon Creek, wide as it is. But these lines hold only if the winds cooperate and if there is water in the streambeds.

The fire crackles and snaps as it descends into Maybeck Valley, searching for more fuel. It doesn't take long for it to reach a circle of tall redwoods. It gobbles several inches of fallen branches and needles lying at the trees' feet. The well-fed flames intensify, growing taller, licking the trunks of the trees and climbing up, up, up to new heights where the wind is still gusting. Flames and firebrands—chunks of burning wood—shoot out in all directions, cracking and popping like Fourth of July fireworks. A large firebrand flies across a small stream like a cannon, touching down on the tinder-dry fuel on the other side and breaching the stream before heading for the line laid down in the soil like a wish for safety. In an instant, another fire is ignited, this one just three miles from the village of Santa Bonita.

TWENTY-FIVE

N o!" Sam yells as Marco turns right out of Maverick's driveway, heading up Joaquin Gully toward the Nuñezes' house.
The hill they'd have to pass through to get to the hospital is
in the other direction. Sam's throat aches from smoke but he shouts
as loudly as he can in his friend's ear. "I need to go to the hospital!"

Marco releases the throttle only slightly as he shakes his head.
"*I* need to go home!" he shouts back.

Sam realizes he didn't really communicate his plan to his
friend—he didn't have time—but there is no way he is not complet-
ing his mission. *Get GB. Get to Mom.*

GB squirms, clearly uncomfortable being sandwiched in his tiny
seat between two yelling boys. Sam squeezes the pup a little tighter,
trying to send a *stay still* message. It just makes the dog wriggle

more. Desperation floods every cell in Sam's body as the ATV continues moving up the hill.

"Marco!" Sam shouts his friend's name as tears spring to his eyes. "Dude!" he begs. If they go back to the Nuñez house, Marco's parents will never let them out of their sight. He needs to get to the hospital. He needs to see his mom, to be with her. How can he explain this?

Sensing all of it, Marco turns to look at his friend. But the moment his eyes leave the road the quad swerves wildly.

"Whoa!" Marco shouts. He jerks the handlebars, overcorrecting. The ATV careens to the right and both of the left-hand wheels rise off the ground. "Hold on!" Marco shouts, his shoulders rising to his ears.

Goodboy lets out a terrified yelp while Sam squeezes Marco's waist, encircling the dog and instinctively leaning the other way to help balance the vehicle.

With a thud, the left-hand wheels slam back onto the ground and the threesome slams right along with them, somehow managing to stay on the seat. *Ouch!* GB is shaking now, and as Marco slows, Sam releases his grip to stroke the dog's shoulder. That was hairy.

Sam stays silent while his heart thuds with residual fear. Part of him wants to yell at Marco, starting with "Dude!" But Marco is doing the best he can, and Sam knows he couldn't do better himself.

Marco lets the throttle go and the ATV rolls to a stop. He turns to look at Sam for a second and Sam watches his chest rise, and then fall—issuing a silent apology. Marco focuses forward once more, gathering his courage to drive. They sit there for several seconds, saying nothing.

"Okay," Marco finally says. It's a reply to Sam's earlier request. Without looking back again, Marco makes a slow, wide turn and heads down the road toward the village, in the direction that Sam wants to go.

Leaning forward, Sam shelters GB and rests his head against Marco's back. He exhales his relief, his gratitude. Somehow GB's tongue finds his face.

Marco accelerates slowly, gathering confidence. He slows around the curves and the three wind their way through the smoky haze toward the village. After a few minutes, Sam raises his head again and looks around. He blinks and tries to determine where they are. His eyes have itched and burned for so long he's almost stopped noticing, but it's difficult to see anything clearly, and right now his eyeballs feel like they've been sanded and nobody blew away the grit.

Still, he can make out enough to tell that the area closer to Santa Bonita must have been evacuated before Cypress Ridge. It is completely, *completely* deserted. There are no cars or people to be seen, just a few skeleton and scarecrow yard decorations that seem waaay more haunting than they did a few days ago. Everything looks bizarre and feels wrong.

"This is . . . creepy," Sam murmurs as they make the turn onto Main Street. None of the streetlights are working, but Marco slows as he approaches each intersection. Sam is grateful that his friend is being careful after almost flipping them, but the irony of being cautious isn't lost on him. After all, there's a massive forest fire bearing down from who knows where—maybe everywhere at once. They are driving a stolen ATV and ignoring citywide evacuation orders. Safety seems like something Sam can only imagine—like a unicorn or a dragon. At the moment, he's not even sure it exists!

Stroking GB's fur, Sam tries to keep calm—for both of them. For all of them.

They pass the last stop sign in town and Marco turns onto the winding back road—too small to have a painted yellow line down the center—that will take them on the slow road over Regina Pass to the hospital. As soon as they're clear of the ninety-degree turn, Marco twists the throttle and they pick up speed. Seeing the ghost town somehow made their mission feel more urgent.

The back road to the hospital is narrower and curvier and way less maintained. The trio bounces along it, and Sam has to tighten his hold on his friend and dog when Marco swerves here and there to avoid small potholes and debris in the road.

"We should've grabbed helmets!" Sam shouts, adding the lack of head protection to his mental list of the day's unsafe behavior. Marco doesn't reply—he just weaves. He navigates the four-wheeler around a fallen tree branch a little too fast.

This time it's the right-hand wheels that lift off the pavement. "Hang on!" Marco half shouts, half coughs out. He does a much more graceful job correcting this time. The wheels touch back down with only a little thud, and almost no loss of speed.

GB whimpers, and Sam buries his nose behind the dog's ear. "It's okay, boy," he tells him, trying to ignore the ever-tightening knots in his stomach. "We just have to hang on."

TWENTY-SIX

Sam isn't sure whether Marco's driving is getting better because he's getting the hang of it, because of survival instinct, or because he's so terrified he's just *going*. The smoke continues to thicken and larger pieces of ash float down from the sky to settle on everything in a ghostly layer. It's like a snowstorm from hell. Riding behind him, Sam keeps his own eyes on the road and leans into the curves to help keep all four wheels on the ground.

Goodboy has stopped squirming between them. Sam hopes he's not smashing his dog like the banana in a peanut-butter-and-banana sandwich. As long as GB stays in the gooey middle and doesn't squish out the sides, maybe everything will be okay.

They don't see a single other vehicle as they travel the back road.

After what seems like forever, they make it back to the county-maintained streets, and then the commercial zone near the hospital. Unlike the village, Sam sees a few cars here and there, parked in the strip malls that line the thoroughfare. But no people. And no lights—the power is out here, too.

The weird, haunted feeling he'd felt in Santa Bonita returns. Ever since the fire started, he's felt as if he's trapped in a zombie apocalypse video game just waiting for the undead to come lurching out of the smoke. Realizing he's probably squeezing the life out of Marco's shoulders, he forces himself to loosen his grip at the same moment he spots some dimly glowing lights in the distance. There's only one thing they can be: the hospital! Bonita General would definitely have generators to keep life-sustaining equipment turned on, even during a power outage.

Sam's heart gives a leap—they are so close! His mom is somewhere in those lights! Then, looking up at the hill that looms over the hospital like a hulking ogre, he spies a flickering line of bright-orange flames on what would be the crown of the ogre's head. The fire is so close to Bonita General it makes Sam's heart lurch as if it would like to escape his chest and get the heck out of here without him.

Marco must see the flames, too, because he lays on the throttle and they tear through the hospital parking lot, heading straight for the ambulance unloading zone. There are hardly any cars in patient parking, and Sam doesn't see a single ambulance in the section of the lot where they're usually parked two deep, waiting for a call.

Sam lets go of Marco, ready to hurl himself off the quad and run straight into the building and, he hopes, his mom's arms. He pictures her sitting in the lounge with her bright yellow clogs up on a chair, eating her all-time favorite Chunky Monkey ice cream. She's laughing with her coworkers, who know not only Sam's name but also waaay too much about him. He'd give anything to walk in there and find exactly that—he'd happily field the comments about how big he's gotten and how handsome he is . . . heck, he'd even take the endless questions about school! But the lack of ambulances suggests that nobody inside is sitting around on breaks, talking, or laughing. Sam swallows. This doesn't look good.

Marco cruises right up the ramp and stops at the sliding doors, where patient arrivals are typically unloading from emergency vehicles and whisked inside on stretchers. A firefighter in a yellow suit with reflective striping is standing in front of the automatic doors, talking into a radio. He gives the boys . . . and dog, a look. It is crystal clear—even with the smoky haze—that he is not happy to see them. He shakes his black-helmeted head and pushes up his face guard.

Sam scrambles off the ATV before it comes to a full stop. GB hops down and scampers after him. They rush toward the entrance, but the firefighter—a big man with a dark mustache and rough hands—grabs Sam's arm, holding him back. He's still talking into his radio. "One second, Rachel," he says. Then he stares at Sam, who looks away.

Goodboy barks, but the bark turns to a whimper when the

firefighter's gaze lowers in his direction. GB sits down at Sam's feet.

"What do you think you guys are doing?" the man asks gruffly. "You can't go in there—the hospital is being evacuated. We're trying to get everybody *out*!"

Sam's blood feels frozen inside his veins. The signs were all there, of course. But he had to hold on to hope. Besides Marco's shoulders, that's all he has!

The fireman studies Sam's face, sees it change. "The fire is coming this way," he says in a softer voice. He points at the hill glowing in the distance, but Sam can't bring himself to look at the threat again. He has seen it. He knows it's there. He knows it's way too close.

"We're just waiting on transportation for the last few patients." The fireman's tone changes again—back to all business. "This area is not safe . . . for anyone. You boys need to get out of here!"

Sam blinks rapidly. His eyes are watering, but he's not crying. He isn't. He's just desperate!

"No. You don't understand. My mom is in there," Sam squeaks. A tear escapes. Okay, maybe he *is* crying. His whole body shudders, and he feels like he might fall over. Goodboy leans into his leg, propping him up as best a dog can. "I need to get to her . . . please. Or at least know where she's gone . . ." Sam is full-on pleading now. Marco appears at his side to back him up, but he doesn't need to say anything.

The man's stern look fades again and he shakes his head. "Rachel, you still there?" he says, raising the radio to his mouth. It crackles. Rachel is there.

"You see any sign of that ambulance?" a woman's voice asks.

"No, listen. I have a kid here who is looking for his mom. Says she's a patient at the—"

"Not a patient," Sam interrupts. It's important to get this right. "My mom works here. Her name is Vivian Durand. She's a PA." *She has to be here*, he thinks. *She has to.*

The man nods his understanding. He repeats Vivian's name into the radio, along with the correction that she's a physician's assistant. He places a hand on Sam's shoulder and this time all three of them look up at the glowing line on the hill, waiting silently for an answer. The radio crackles again and again, but no voice sounds. Sam holds his breath for what feels like forever. *Please, please, please*, he thinks. *Please, please, please, please, please.*

CHAPTER
TWENTY-SEVEN

The doe stands with her fawn in a large pool in the southern section of Falcon Creek. The pool is familiar. The twosome often comes here to drink and rest in the shade. In fact, the doe gave birth in a thicket not far away. Today, though, they're here for something else—refuge. They are here to escape the heat and smoke and flames that have been creeping closer for days, and now seem to surround them on all sides. They've been standing in the creek for hours. The fawn's slim legs tremble.

Other animals have also come to the creek seeking shelter and relief. Predator and prey alike have put aside their instincts to focus on one thing: survival. Raccoons crouch on the shore. A family of quail huddle under a bush. A bobcat with a singed coat crouches in the shallows near the bank, submerging as much of her body as she can next to a piece of driftwood. A fox wades back and forth, back and forth, never stopping to clamber onto dry land. Other, smaller creatures hide in crevices and stumps and wait for the fire to pass . . . or to take them.

The cool, dark water—which isn't moving fast like it does in spring—flows quietly downstream. The deer balance in the deepest section of the pool, their cloven hooves perched on the waterlogged sticks and river rocks that cover the bottom. Their ears stand upright, on alert. They do not dare dip their heads to drink. The usually clear stream is filled with black ash and charred pieces of wood that have fallen or blown in and drifted downstream to bob in their tainted watering hole.

Fire burns on both sides of the ravine now. It roars in the wind, trying to outshout the chopping blades of the helicopters that circle above. The sounds make the doe flinch. Her ears flick constantly, trying to twitch the noise away. It's much too constant, too loud.

Suddenly there's a loud crack from high overhead. A burning branch crashes down from the bower of a tall tree farther upstream. It smashes into other branches on the way down, snapping them, spreading flames, and adding to the terrible noise. The already spooked fawn goes rigid for a split second, then bolts, desperate for an escape. She tears out of the water, her slender spotted body frantic to *get away*. She races up the bank and, in her terror, sprints toward the heart of the danger.

CHAPTER

TWENTY-EIGHT

The radio is silent for what seems like forever. It takes all Sam's will not to grab it out of the firefighter's hand and start shouting into it. *Where is my mom? Has she been evacuated? I need to get to her now! She's all the family I have!* He must look as unhinged as he feels, because Marco gets between him and the firefighter with the mustache and starts talking to Sam in his calm voice.

"Hey. Do you have any water in there?" Marco nods at the pack Sam had almost forgotten was on his back. "Goodboy is probably pretty thirsty."

Gooodboy. Yes. The dog is still leaning into his calf, but Sam was so distracted he didn't really feel it. He removes the pack, grateful for something to do, and for his dog. He squats down, pours a small amount of water into his cupped hand, and offers it to Goodboy. GB barely sniffs it. He just lets out another whimper and leans harder into Sam, who digs deeper into the pack for one of his pup's favorite treats. "Here, boy," he says. Sam holds the bone-shaped biscuit under his dog's nose. Usually, just reaching for the treat container is enough to unleash a river of anticipatory drool from Goodboy's mouth. But now GB turns away.

"I feel ya," Sam says, pocketing the treat as yet another lump grows in his stomach. Even his dog knows how awful this situation is. He thumps GB's side. He can't imagine trying to force down the cereal bar he's been carrying since this morning, or biting into one of the apples in his pack. *Wow.* That was just this morning! It doesn't seem possible.

Not eating and drinking are signs of distress for sure—especially for a chowhound like Goodboy. And the pup is demonstrating a third sign of fear, too. With each thump to his side, a cloud of hair erupts from GB's flank. Sam's pants are *covered* in dog hair, too—the dog is a shed machine. He's doing something called "blowing coat" or stress shedding—something Sam learned about when Goodboy practically shed himself bald when he got his first shots.

Sam runs his hand over GB's fur, generating yet another pile of hair, while Marco pulls out his phone and starts pressing buttons. Sam takes out his own phone in case the service is different here, but there's still no signal and all the messages to his mom are still right there on the screen. UNDELIVERED . . . even though she might be just a few hundred yards away!

When the radio finally crackles to life, Sam jumps and stands up.

"PA Durand was evacuated with a group of patients about an hour ago," Rachel reports over the radio, confirming that Sam's mom is not inside the hospital.

"Where did they go?" Sam blurts, impatient. His voice is hoarse, and the security guy holds out a hand to quiet him. Rachel isn't finished talking.

"The ambulance she was in evacuated to Cross Memorial," she reports through the radio.

The fireman nods as he listens. "Thanks, I'll direct them from here." The radio clicks off, then goes silent. The man is silent, too, taking in the boys, the four-wheeler, the dog. His mustache twitches the slightest bit. He takes a deep breath and gives them a look that says "I hope I don't regret this," before finally speaking.

"You boys have a good amount of gas in that vehicle?" the fireman asks, directing the question at Marco, the driver. *That's smart*, Sam thinks. Because he has no idea. Plus, Marco seems to be keeping it together waaay better than he is!

"Yes," Marco replies, nodding. "It still has three quarters of a tank, though I don't exactly know how far that will take us."

The firefighter's mustache twitches again. "Probably sixty miles, give or take," he replies. "Should be far enough." Then he turns to Sam. "I know you want to get to your mom," he says as his voice drops low. "But the road from here to Crown is too dangerous now." He pauses, then repeats, "*Too dangerous*."

Sam blinks and shifts uncomfortably. He wants to turn away,

but the emergency worker holds his eyes with a laser stare.

"We've got multiple fires burning and moving fast. They are hot as hell, and equally unpredictable. Trying to get to Crown would be a death sentence." He holds Sam's gaze for another several seconds. "Do you understand?"

Sam swallows back tears and nods, not trusting his voice. Finally, the firefighter releases him from his arresting gaze and Sam gulps again.

"Okay," the man looks back at Marco and points in the direction they just arrived from. "You need to go back the way you came, through town and up over Regina Pass to the village." He shakes his head and an expression flickers over his face, almost as if it hurts him to send them back. "I think you can make it out on Joaquin Gulley." He gestures again, in the same direction. "That's the safest route out. But you can't waste a single second," he orders. "Drive as fast as you can. Be safe, but hurry. I don't know how much longer you're going to be able to get through." He hesitates one final time. "Okay!" he says. "Go! Now!"

Sam and Marco don't need to be told twice. They turn and cover the distance to the ATV in less than three seconds. Sam scrambles aboard, pulling Goodboy up in front of him. The sturdy, muscular dog feels almost limp, a fact Sam tries hard to ignore as Marco starts the engine. The Honda rumbles.

"Wait!" the man shouts, moving toward them. "Take these." He's holding fabric in his hands, and Sam wonders where the heck he got it . . . it's not as if there's a pile of bed sheets lying by the hospital door. Could it be from his own shirt? Whatever it is, the firefighter rips the cloth into two large strips and then douses them both with bottled water before holding them out to the boys.

Sam takes them, understanding. These are makeshift masks, to cover their mouths and noses and help keep out the smoke particles. He coughs while he ties his on, kicking himself for not thinking of it earlier. Marco watches for a second, takes his strip, and follows suit, covering his own airways. There's not much they can do for GB.

"That should help filter the smoke," the man says before slapping the back of the ATV, hard. "Now get out of here!"

TWENTY-NINE

The visibility of the road in front of the speeding ATV is hazy at best, and more debris has blown in and scattered across the roadway. It's like an obstacle course. Conditions are worsening rapidly. As Sam squints into the near distance, he isn't sure if he wants his friend to speed up or slow down! The smoke makes it hard to see more than ten feet in front of them, and though the wet cloth must be helping, it isn't offering any actual relief. The air still burns his nose and throat, even through his makeshift mask.

Marco swerves, and the boys tilt to the right in unison. Sam swears GB leans right along with them, even though he still seems pretty listless and weak—at least compared to his usual wiggly self. After crossing Regina Pass, they roll down the hill and make the turn off the back road and onto Main Street of the Santa Bonita village, following the path of their last scary ride, but in reverse. This time, Macro rolls through the stop signs and the dark intersections. They blow through block after block without slowing at all.

Sam turns his head and presses his cheek against his friend's back. He squeezes his stinging eyes shut for a second. When he opens them, he's looking at Inside Scoop—and he sees something move through the window!

"Wait! Stop!" Sam shouts, hoping to be heard through his wet mask and over the Honda's engine. "We have to stop!"

Marco lays on the brakes and they come to a quick halt, but when he turns to look at Sam, his expression is tense . . . mad, even. "Dude! You heard what the firefighter said. We—"

Sam points at the ice cream shop, and Marco's dark eyes widen. "Ay!" he says. Through the haze, they can just make out Esther Hightower's wrinkly face peering out at them from between a pair of red-and-white checkered curtains.

"What is she doing here?" Sam mutters.

Marco is off the ATV first. Sam and GB hurry after him, all of them heading for the closed door of the shop. Esther is still peeking out the window and Sam starts to pull down his mask so she can see who he is, and immediately begins to cough.

"It's us!" Marco shouts needlessly.

The door to the shop opens. "I know who you are!" Esther says from the doorway. She starts to cough, too, and holds her arm over her face, her mouth tucked into the elbow.

The boys wait for her to speak, but GB doesn't wait for anything! At the sight of Esther, he perks up to his normal energy level and starts full-body wagging. He hops on his two back feet, trying to reach Esther's hand to give it a lick. At the same time, the sneaky devil attempts to squeeze past her into the shop. Esther's pup cups—frozen custards just for dogs—have cast a permanent spell on GB and earned Esther a dog devotee for life!

"No, no," Esther says as she comes out of the coughing fit. She positions herself just so, blocking GB from moving farther into the shop. "You can't come in. In fact, all three of you have to get out of here right away! We've been evacuated, you know." Esther's gray braids—usually twisted into a bun—swish around her shoulders as she shakes her head.

"We know—we were on our way out when we spotted you. Why are *you* still here?" Sam asks pointedly.

Esther's shoulders lift toward her ears and she looks slightly embarrassed. "I started to leave, but my gas tank is almost empty. By the time I realized I didn't have enough gas to get out of town, Jerry had already closed the station and everyone was gone. I figure I'm better off here than on the side of the road needing to be rescued! I don't think the fire is going to come to Main Street, anyway."

Marco and Sam exchange a brief but meaningful look. There is no way they are leaving Esther in her store.

"You can't stay here," Marco insists. "None of us can. You're coming with us." He has his hand on his head, a handful of hair in his fist. He looks like he's literally trying to pull an idea out of his brain. Mr. Nuñez does the same thing when he's thinking . . . and stressed.

Esther looks past the boys to the Honda and then back at the boys . . . her loyal customers. "Oh no, don't you go worrying about me!" she insists. "That looks like a bicycle built for two and I have plenty of melting ice cream to keep me occupied. Like I said, I'll be fine."

Marco shakes his head emphatically.

"You're definitely coming with us," Sam says, even as his brain asks him how this is even possible.

All three of them turn and stare at the small vehicle—their only transportation. Esther is pretty slight, but Goodboy is stout for a dog. There's just no way they'll all fit.

Having given up on the pup cup, GB whines softly at their feet. Sam feels like whining, too. He lets his head drop back, forcing his gaze upward at the grimy sky. Then suddenly, out of the corner of his eye, he sees a flash of orange. He turns quickly, zeroing in, and catches another flicker up on the ridge.

Atop the ridge south of Regina Pass, the fire is visible and closing in! Sam stares, transfixed. It's . . . right . . . there!

Following Sam's terrified gaze, Esther and Marco see it, too.

"Sam!" Marco shouts. "Climb onto the cargo rack!"

The small rack isn't large enough to fit Goodboy, let alone Sam. But even if Sam could become some sort of easily stowed cargo, there's still not enough room.

Sam adjusts his backpack, racking his brain, and suddenly gets an idea. GB is stout—but also kind of compact.

"Hold on," Sam pushes past Marco and Esther and steps into the ice cream shop. "I have an idea that I think will work!" He hurries behind the counter and begins to unload his backpack. He takes out everything, laying it all out on the counter. The food. The first aid. The two bottles of water.

The last thing he pulls out is his dad's camera. He pulls it from the case and gently unwraps it. He sets it down on the counter and rests his palm on it for just a second, feeling the hard metal body, the curved lens. "I'm sorry, Dad," he whispers. "We have to save Esther, and we can't save her *and* your camera. She matters more."

"Sam!" Marco shouts from outside.

"I'm coming," Sam says, still in a whisper. He snatches up one of the water bottles and the apples and shoves them into the side pocket of the pack, then grabs a dish towel from the stack Esther always has at the ready for spills and cleanups. He wets it in the sink and races outside. "Here!" Sam thrusts the damp towel at Esther to use for a mask.

"GB, come!" Sam calls. The dog is already at his feet. "Now comes the tricky part. Marco, can you help?"

Stooping down, with Marco supporting GB's middle, Sam fits his dog's hind legs into the backpack and then starts to pull it up like a sleeping bag around his round, furry body. The pit bull is amazingly compliant, and Sam has a flash of him wearing Sofia's silly costumes. Maybe the two of them had been practicing for an emergency all along!

"Okay, now help me get him on my back!" Sam says.

Marco lifts the stuffed pup and Sam slides his arms into the straps. GB rests one paw on each of Sam's shoulders and pants in his ear. It works! Goodboy is ready to roll and won't take up an inch of seat space.

"I'll ride in back," Sam says, directing Esther, who has secured her wet dish towel mask.

Marco is already on the ATV and revving as Esther lifts her leg over the seat behind him. Climbing on board, Sam completes the ice cream queen sandwich. The metal of the cargo rack is hard beneath his tailbone and GB's claws dig painfully into his shoulders, but Sam doesn't care. They're all on and ready to get the heck out of here!

Marco steers them out of the village, turns onto Joaquin Gully, and takes them on a nightmare version of their familiar bike route.

"Hang on!" he shouts, but Esther is already clinging to her driver for dear life.

Before they make the turn out of town, Sam looks back to see the fire on the other edge of the village eating its way down the coastal mountain, moving ever closer. He swallows hard as dread and adrenaline swirl in a whirling vortex inside him. He grasps Esther's small frame, and Marco guns it.

CHAPTER
THIRTY

Within five minutes it's clear that they are not going to get over Cypress Ridge before the fire reaches it. Or them. They can see the glow ahead, and to the south as well. It feels as if everything is converging. One second they're racing forward as fast as the quad can go, and then, suddenly, the vehicle comes to a dead stop.

"We're not going to get through," Marco says.

"Drat!" Esther cries, shaking a bony fist.

Sam blinks as if it will help him see his friend more clearly. As if it will do any good at all. He wishes with every fiber of his being that he could disagree. But there's no arguing with the giant orange monster roaring all around them, lurching ever closer.

Sweat runs down Sam's back. His face is smeared with soot from debris and falling ash. All three of their faces glisten with perspiration from the mad heat.

Sam tries to think. He looks over one shoulder, then the other. He has lived in the Santa Bonita hills his whole life. He knows every bump, creek, and trail. He racks his brain. Where can they go? Where can they find safety?

He gives his head a little shake, a trick he picked up from Goodboy. It helps clear his head. The bike trail he took from Marco's isn't far away. It's not a quad track—it's narrow. The going will be rough, and parts of it might not be passable. But out past his house, it does wind through a rocky, canyon-like section of Falcon Creek. It's the best option he can think of.

He turns to Marco, a glimmer of hope rising in his chest. "Little Yosemite?" Most of the time, the majority of Santa Bonita kids are forbidden from visiting the rocky ravine named after the famous national park. It's considered dangerous, especially during spring, when water rushes over the boulders, creating waterfalls and rapids that look like a tiny version of the cascades in the real Yosemite. That rushing water worries parents, and also creates rock-lined hollows . . . hollows that have been dried up during the past few drought years.

Hollows that might save their butts from a raging forest fire.

"That's single track," Marco replies. He sounds so tired. So defeated. So unlike Marco.

But Esther is nodding hard. "We can do it!" Her voice is surprisingly strong coming through her towel mask. "It's our only chance," she adds, her voice quieter. Her bright, wrinkly blue eyes dart from one boy to the other.

Marco's gaze travels from their unlikely passenger to Sam, and then to Goodboy, who is panting in Sam's ear. Sam is okay with the heavy breathing—he'd choose his dog's stinky breath over wildfire smoke any day.

Finally, Marco nods. "Okay," he says. "Little Yosemite it is." He spins around, planting his butt back on the seat and pushing the quad's handlebars as far left as they can go. The ATV veers and doubles back. Marco drives s-l-o-w-l-y along the left side of the road. Sam squints hard, his eyes peeled, searching for the trail.

"I see it!" Esther's slender hand lets go of Marco's shoulder to point. Sure enough, the trail is right there, snaking away from the road into the woods. The earth and trees here are untouched by the fire . . . so far. But the blaze is roaring downhill, heading right for them. The heat is crazy intense. Sam wonders how long it will be before he feels his skin begin to sizzle like steak on a grill. He closes his eyes for a moment, a silent prayer, as Marco drives them all off the road.

As expected, the trail is too tight for the ATV, and it's rough going. "Sorry!" Marco shouts back at his passengers, who have to deflect branches while trying to stay on board.

"We're fine," Esther yells back. "Just go!"

Marco accelerates hard. Sam squeezes Esther tighter. They roar up the trail, the ATV skimming between rocks and trees. It's like being in a video game!

"Lean right!" Marco coughs out. Sam pulls Esther's shoulders to the right side of the Honda as they blast between a bus-size boulder and a stand of pines, the rock missing their legs by mere inches. No sooner are they back upright when they hear another order from the driver's seat.

"Duuuuck!"

Sam bends himself forward, willing all of them—especially Goodboy—to be as tiny as possible as they scrape underneath a fallen (but, thankfully, not burning) tree.

"Woof!" GB's bark is plaintive, begging.

"Hold on, boy!" Sam shouts, letting go of Esther with one hand to give his dog a quick pat on the head. They roll over a rock, which sends all of them momentarily up off their seats.

"These things should come with seat belts!" Sam shouts as flickers of orange pervade his peripheral vision. He turns slightly and wishes he hadn't. Fire burns to the left—and ahead. He can't tell how far away it is, but it's definitely too close.

Faster, he thinks, closing his eyes. *Drive faster.* It feels like he's inside the fire—he can hear it, feel it, taste it. His eyes water behind his closed eyelids. His lungs ache.

Suddenly, the engine stops, and Sam opens his eyes.

"I don't think I can get any closer." Marco's voice is so hoarse that Sam can barely understand him, but it is obvious there is only one thing to do . . .

"Go, go, go!" Esther shouts through her towel.

They clamber off the ATV and run toward Little Yosemite

through what feels like a tunnel of orange, gray, and black. Sam can picture the large rock that hangs over the creek bed—he's jumped off it into the water dozens of times, despite warnings from his mom—but he cannot see it. He can't see anything but smoke and fire.

Just as Marco gets to the edge of the creek, two flaming pine trees fall to their right, shooting a line of flames in their direction. *Whoooosh!*

Sparks fly as Marco jumps the eight feet into the boulder-filled creek bed. He looks like a superhero in the gray-orange light. As soon as he lands, he reaches up for Esther, who is quick to follow, after peering over the edge and making sure the coast is clear.

Sam pauses, afraid. There is no water in there—nothing to break his fall, and he's carrying twenty extra pounds on his back. *Kaboom!* Something else explodes, and a giant whoosh of hot air blasts Sam and GB from behind.

"Hold on, boy!" he shouts to GB, and leaps.

THIRTY-ONE

The fawn races up the trail, her eyes watering, her vision blurred. She stumbles, unable to see more than a few feet in front of her. Flames lick the trees and sky all around—hot smears of orange. The heat is everywhere, pressing in as she runs. It makes her dizzy but she doesn't stop. She doesn't slow. She runs, the smell of burnt fur wafting off her tawny, speckled coat. Her tongue licks the end of her cracked black snout. It tastes of dried blood.

The fawn is so thirsty. She lapped up a few sips of water from the creek while her mother kept watch, but it wasn't enough to quench her endless thirst. Plus, the water didn't taste fresh and clean like it usually does. It tasted like fire.

The young deer races onward, her legs leaping over rocks and blackened logs that litter the forest floor. She trips over a toppled log and falls. Landing hard, the wind in her lungs disappears. It takes several minutes for her to come to her senses and get back on her feet. She moves on, a little more slowly now, her body aching and rigid with fear. She. Is. So. Tired.

Finally, the fawn finds herself at the edge of a streambed scattered with giant boulders. She sniffs, trying to detect the scent of water. Yes! It's faint, but it is there. She's scrambling down for a drink when a burning branch falls from the sky, landing in a shower of spark and flame. *Kaboom!* Something explodes just behind her. She lurches forward.

The streambed holds nothing but dry pebbles. There was water here once, but it's gone now. The fawn longs to lie down, to rest, but she can feel her mother urging her on in her head—urging her to find shelter, safety . . . Moving unsteadily, the fawn makes her way to a small opening beneath a granite overhang.

"Ahhhhh!"

"Woooooff!"

Sam and Goodboy land hard, thankfully just enough on top of Marco to break their fall without injuring him. Marco gets to his feet immediately.

"We've got to get to that big outcropping!" he shouts.

Sam helps Esther to her feet and they all follow Marco as he picks his way across the dry streambed. Sam's gone only a few steps when he misplaces his foot, and his ankle twists, scraping against a jagged river rock. GB lets out a low whimper as if just for him. Sam limps forward, trying to keep up, ignoring the pain.

Only a handful of feet above them and a hundred feet away, the fire devours everything it can reach, burning through the scrubby brush at the edges of Falcon Creek. Between the fear and the smoke, Sam can barely breathe.

"Come on!" Marco's voice chokes out somewhere up ahead in the smoky haze.

Another tree falls from up the hill, showering them with bright orange sparks. Sam can feel them burning through his clothes. He lunges forward with a final push, landing with the others beneath the rocky outcropping at the far side of the creek. The massive basalt shelf acts as a kind of roof, and the four of them squeeze against the back of the nature-made lean-to in a huddle, hoping it will be enough to protect them.

Just outside the opening, flaming branches and trees break and fall while the fires burn closer. Sam's ankle throbs, but the pain is nothing next to the fear. Is this a shelter or a trap? He prays that it's the first of the two.

GB licks Sam's ear obsessively, still strapped to his back. Nobody speaks. Sam focuses on his dog, taking off his pack and swinging it around to wear it on his front. Now GB is basically on his lap. Sam is just grateful for something to hold on to.

Esther lets out a long, ragged cough. The tips of her braids are blackened with soot. The air in the little ravine is the tiniest bit cooler than it was above. Sam tries his best to breathe, but shallowly. He can't block out the terrifying sound of the inferno. It roars so loud that part of Sam tells himself to flee—to get out—even after they worked so hard to get *in*.

Over the deafening roar, Sam hears the bass boom of a large

propane tank exploding, making it sound even more like a war is being waged. He is vaguely aware that there are no more helicopter noises, and wonders if it's because fighting the fire has become a lost cause.

Sam pushes that thought away and pulls GB tighter into his lap, presses his shoulder into Marco's, and closes his eyes. There's nothing to do now but wait. Wait, and hope.

THIRTY-THREE

The afternoon winds urge the fire on. It blasts up hilly inclines, racing to the summits, leaving nothing but scorched earth in its wake.

Having done what they can in the wilderness, Gabi and her crew are now focused on doing all they can to protect homes and businesses. Exhausted and demoralized by the fire's strength and traveling speed, they work on a residential subdivision, hoping to save homes. Some houses stand a better chance than others because their owners removed fallen leaves and pine needles from their rooftops and gutters, trimmed overhanging branches, and cleared dead and dying shrubs and plants away from the walls . . . all before the fire started. Other homes are in severe danger.

Her face dripping with sweat, Gabi hoists a lawn chair over her shoulder. Her face shield helps keep her safe, but the heat is relentless. She delivers the chair to a pile several hundred feet from a house, then goes back for another. And another. She detaches a propane tank from a gas grill and carries it to another heap. Nearby, the buzz of a chain saw mingles with the hissing and whirring and cracking of the fire as a fellow crew member cuts lower limbs from pine trees growing close to the house. If they can keep the fire from reaching the crowns of the trees—and spewing embers and firebrands down onto the roofs—it will keep the blaze from spreading quickly and doing more damage.

Gabi can both hear and feel the fire coming. She knows from reports that it's burning toward the commercial and residential neighborhoods of Santa Bonita all at once. Other crews are working to save other dwellings, as well as Main Street in the village. Everyone is hoping that the fire will change its path. That the wind will change direction and begin blowing in from the sea—blowing the fire back toward the area it has already consumed so that it will starve and dwindle out. Everyone knows that hope is fleeting.

Gabi climbs a ladder to a rooftop and begins to hurriedly sweep it clear of pine needles. On the ground, a few firefighters ready hoses to spray down rooftops. If a structure catches, there's not much they can do. With a fire this strong and hot, if a building catches, it can be engulfed in five minutes. In less than an hour, there could be nothing left but stone stairs, brick fireplaces, smoldering ashes, and pools of aluminum.

Gabi recognized her aunt's and uncle's street when they passed it an hour ago. Or was it three hours? She is both grateful and distressed that she wasn't assigned to that particular neighborhood. She tries not to think about family when she's on the job. She has work to do.

From the rooftop, she sees flames flickering in the valley, possibly near Main Street, though she can't see any more detail than that. But not too far away, she recognizes the tall flames and acrid smells of a structure burning as the fire takes a house, then another, while leaving a third home standing between them mercifully and inexplicably unscathed.

Between swipes with her industrial broom, Gabi prays.

THIRTY-FOUR

We're going to be okay," Marco yells over the roar of the fire. Sam isn't sure if he's trying to convince him, or Esther, or himself. Probably all three.

"Yes, we are," Esther agrees through her wet towel. Once clean and white, it's now a bleak gray. "Yes, we are."

Sam's throat clenches and he holds tight to GB, who has begun to shake worse than he does during Fourth of July fireworks. He's lost so much hair it's a wonder he isn't bald.

In the streambed just outside the little rock lean-to, bits of orange flash in a muddle of thick gray. The sound of crashing branches is nearly nonstop. Sam doesn't want to look but can't seem to stop himself from craning his neck to peer into the inferno. He spies flames licking the treetops above them like a giant orange tongue, then buries his face in GB's neck again. It's better when he keeps his eyes closed.

"It's going to pass," Marco says, over and over. "We are going to be okay."

Sam's entire body is covered in sweat, as if he's been sitting in a hot sauna. He is about to agree with Marco, when a terrible roar—the loudest they've heard—thunders from all directions. Half a second later, an unimaginable blast of heat engulfs the space around them, sucking out the air, drying the sweat. Sam's lungs feel like a deflated balloon and he fears taking a breath.

He breathes in. The air is so hot it burns.

A blinding flash of orange light illuminates the little cave as brightly as a stage during a rock concert. Sam counts the seconds, burying his head in his arms and trying to hold his searing breath until he has to let it out. He tries to do it slowly, but has no control. The scorching inhale afterward hurts more than anything he's felt in his life. He holds his breath again, waiting, his lungs burning and bursting all at once. In his lap, GB is shaking and silent—which is somehow worse than the whimpering. His dog is hurting. Sam keeps a hand on his head. It's all he has to give.

Just when Sam can't hold his breath a moment longer, the sound begins to change and the light dims. He exhales solidly, and then slooowly inhales. It's still awful, but not as bad this time.

Gradually, the roar begins to fade. It's moving away. Taking its time. Nobody makes a sound.

The foursome waits, tense and still. They breathe in near-silent unison until the roar is almost undetectable. Then they wait some more.

"I think that was it," Marco finally says. "I think we survived."

Esther croaks out a half laugh. "Let's hope so."

GB starts to squirm and whimper again, as if he can't stay still a moment longer. Sam loosens his grip, too shocked to do much of anything, and the pup wriggles free of the pack and races out of the shelter.

"GB!" Sam yells. Before he can get to his feet, GB yelps and runs back, landing in Sam's lap. He starts whining loudly, frantically licking the pads on his front paws.

"Those rocks have to be five hundred degrees," Marco says.

Sam nods as he checks his dog's pads. They are hardened and hot (!) but not blistering . . . yet. He wishes he had ice. He wishes there was something he could do! They're sitting in an oven, and just outside their little cave, it is set to HOT.

"We'll just have to wait," Esther announces. "And hope the rocks cool down enough for us to get out of here."

Sam knows Esther is right, even though it's the last thing he wants to hear. He wants to *go*. He has to get out of here, to find his mom. And what if the fire comes back? Logically he knows this won't happen. The fire has already consumed the fuel here. It has passed, and it won't return. But fear is still crawling around his brain like a termite infestation.

Sam leans back, half against Marco and half against the rock of the shelter.

"Dude," Marco whispers hoarsely.

Sam waits for more words to come out of his best friend's mouth, but none do. Sam leans farther into his friend, nodding.

"Dude."

There is nothing else to say.

CHAPTER
THIRTY-FIVE

Sam stirs awake from a half sleep. There's something moving tentatively nearby. He opens his bleary eyes and sees Esther outside their rock shelter, gingerly testing the heat of the streambed rocks. She looks like a great blue heron doing a dance. Sam almost laughs out loud at the sight, but realizes his mouth is bone dry and filled with ashy grit. He pulls the water bottle out of the side pocket of his pack and holds out his hand, offering to rewet the cloths covering Marco and Esther's mouths and noses. As soon as the cloth is off his own face, Sam can feel that, while the fire has burned through, a lot of smoke and heat remain. After resecuring his cloth, he offers everyone a few sips. The water is hot but tastes delicious. Sam tries to hold each sip in his mouth for as long as he can before swallowing. They share the apples, which are bruised but taste like something from heaven.

"I think it's cool enough," Ester reports, pushing a braid off her shoulder. "Oh look, I've got raven hair again!" She lets out an amused sniff, noticing that her once-silver plait is black. She slumps back down while Marco helps Sam get GB back into the pack. The dog has gone limp again. They are all dehydrated and drained.

A few moments later, the ragged foursome is standing in the creek bed. What greets their eyes is a hellscape. Scorched earth. Skeletal trees. Smoke rising from small pockets. It's like they're standing in a volcano after it has blown.

They cross back the way they came, looking for a way up the bank on the other side.

"I think we can get up over there," Marco says, pointing to a charred area. The landmarks they might have noticed on the way down are gone, save the massive jumping rock. "No matter what, we have to climb."

The bottoms of their shoes have already melted slightly on the hot rock. They don't offer much in the way of traction but at least protect their feet. Marco leads the way, with Esther in the middle, and Sam bringing up the rear carrying GB in the pack. They move slowly, pulling their shirtsleeves down to use like hot pads on the scorching handholds.

Sam hauls himself up to a little ledge and plants his foot. His ankle throbs in pain, and he remembers the sprain. How could he have forgotten? He shakes his head, befuddled. The brain is so weird.

Before long they're standing at the top of the bank, looking down into the streambed—their refuge. Turning, they try to find the path. Trees and brush still smolder and burn. Pieces of papery ash drift on the air, and the air is still smoky. But the walls of flame are gone. And they are . . . *fine*. Sam blinks back tears of relief. He's never been so happy to be "fine" in his life.

Esther is teary, too. "Thank you, thank you, thank you," she tells the boys. "You saved me." She reaches her arms wide and they come together, squeezing one another in a long hug that includes the bagged-up pit-bull mix.

When they step apart, Sam looks up. The skies remain heavy with smoke. He can't tell exactly where the sun is but knows it will be setting soon, taking the dim light with it. "It'll be dark before we know it," he says. "We've got to keep moving."

Nobody needs to be told twice. The group picks their way along what they hope is the trail they rode in on. Confirmation comes when they spot a strange blocky shape ahead—the burned skeleton of Maverick's quad!

"Holy cow!" Marco exclaims, his eyes riveted on the stolen vehicle. The ATV has been completely destroyed.

"Well said, dude," Sam replies. "Well said."

"Nothing to be done about that," Esther says, nudging them onward. "Keep walking." They move as fast as they can while avoiding smoldering hazards. Everything is hot, but in a different way than before the fire burned through. It feels less scary, but oddly more intense. The heat seeps through the soles of Sam's shoes, burning the bottoms of his feet.

As they continue to trudge up the trail, fatigue sets in. Marco moves slower and slower.

"You okay?" Sam asks. Marco doesn't answer—he trudges unsteadily forward.

Sam worries that they might not make it to the road. *What if his shoes catch fire? What of Marco needs to be carried? Or Esther? How much farther is it?* The questions flap around in his brain, beating against the sides like trapped moths. He's walked and biked this trail a hundred times, but he can't tell where they are, or how much farther they need to go.

Esther trips on a rock and starts to tumble. Somehow, Sam is able to steady her. And then . . .

Suddenly they're at the road. It feels like a miracle. If Sam had a single ounce of energy left, he would cheer, but he doesn't. None of them do.

They are stumbling toward town when they see the headlights of a CAL FIRE truck coming toward them. Another miracle.

The driver eases the truck to a stop when it reaches them. When he climbs out of the cab, Sam recognizes the firefighter who sent them back over Regina Pass. His face breaks into a huge smile, lifting his mustache. But the grin is quickly replaced by something unidentifiable but much more serious.

"Am I glad to see you two . . . I mean three," he says, approaching Esther first and taking her gently by the elbow.

"Yeah, we picked up a passenger," Marco manages to croak out.

The emergency worker situates Esther in the cab first, and then squeezes the boys and GB in, too. It's almost as tight as the ride on the ATV.

"This feels kind of familiar," Marco quips tiredly as Sam's shoulder jabs him in the chest and Sam clutches his backpack full of dog.

"Regina Pass isn't open to regular traffic, but it's clear enough for me to get you to the evacuation center at the county fairgrounds," the firefighter says, starting the truck.

The words *evacuation center* wake Sam up a little. Could his mom be there? *Please please please*, he thinks. *Please let my mom be there* . . .

"They'll be there," Marco says quietly.

"They?" Sam is momentarily confused. His mom is only one person.

"My family," Marco replies, turning to look directly at his friend. His eyes flash for an intense moment, and then Marco turns away.

CHAPTER
THIRTY-SIX

The truck pulls up to the entrance to the fairgrounds and Sam's heart sinks. The place is mobbed. He scans the huge parking lot and scattered buildings but sees no details—only clusters of people huddled together, intermingled with individuals making their way through the scene like zombies. He instantly knows he fits into the zombie category.

A hastily made banner that reads THANK YOU, FIREFIGHTERS hangs on the chain-link fence beside a woman with a walkie-talkie, who is directing cars coming into the lot. She stops each one, leaning in the window, before stepping back and pointing to where they should go. While she talks to a couple pulling a horse trailer, the firefighter who picked them up pulls to the side of the entrance—he doesn't need to take his vehicle in—and helps the boys and Esther out of the cab. Sam instantly starts to scan faces through the chain link.

"I have to head back out to look for survivors," the firefighter says. "But you'll be safe here." He looks at Marco and Sam. "Get some water, and stick with your grandma—you need each other."

Neither Sam nor Marco bother to correct him. Esther isn't related to either of them. And all Sam can think about is finding his mom.

"I see Hank!" Esther says, and immediately moves toward a group of elderly adults not far away.

Marco starts to follow, reminding her that she needs water. But he seems dazed and distracted, too.

Sam adjusts GB, putting him back on his back. He doesn't want him to walk on burnt paws. He skirts the walkie-talkie woman and her clipboard and enters the grounds, uncertain about where to go next.

His ankle throbs. Now that he's safe, the pain is back. He ignores it as best he can and limps toward the buildings.

There! Sam spots three ambulances parked near the door of one of the exhibit halls. Maybe they're using it for injured people. Another hall is being used for food; Sam sees people coming in and out, carrying plates and bottles. Red Cross volunteers are taking cots into the largest building, and Sam guesses that's where people will sleep. He decides that the medical hall is where he's most likely to find his mom.

All around him, filthy, tattered, and utterly worn-out people mill, searching or sobbing or simply wandering in shock. As Sam moves toward a large knot of people, dizziness washes over him like a wave. He is so overwhelmed. He should sit down, rest. But he can't. He makes his way over to the ambulances, searching. He asks if anyone has seen Vivian Durand. Some people can't even answer. Others shake their heads. She isn't there.

From somewhere nearby—he can't quite tell where—he hears Marco shout. "Sam! Over here!"

Sam turns, his aching lungs rising with hope, and sees Marco running toward a small cluster of people. He sees Mr. and Mrs. Nuñez and Sofia. He takes a single step, then stops. From a distance, he watches the family reunite. They are there, together— all four of them—hugging and crying and laughing. Together.

Sam swallows back bile while tears spring to his eyes.

He has never felt so alone in his life.

CHAPTER
THIRTY-SEVEN

Marco is watching Sam over Anita's shoulder, giving him a look so severe that Sam can read it from a distance. But he's unable to move. He knows he should go over to the Nuñezes, say hello. Hug them all. Tell them how happy he is to see them—and how sorry he is for worrying them. That he's glad they're all safe. But his legs and feet are superglued. All he can do is watch.

After a couple minutes, Marco pulls away from his family and comes over. "Dude, what gives?" he says. "Come say hi. My parents want to see you."

Unable to form words, Sam just shakes his head. Marco watches his face. His eyes are confused, then kind . . .

Then full of anger.

His whole face bunches up with frustration. He steps forward, getting close to his friend.

"Sam Durand," he begins. "I'm not sure what is going on with you, but I just scared the living daylights out of my family. And I didn't do that for me . . . I did it for you." Marco stops and looks away, back at his family, before going on. "I picked *you* and *your dog* over *my own family*." His eyes are welling up.

Marco steps back then, taking a breath and wiping his soot-smeared face with his shirtsleeve. He looks Sam in the eye, waiting. Sam holds his friend's gaze for half a second, then drops his eyes. He doesn't know what to say. Or think. Or feel. All he can do is stand there.

Marco exhales long and low and ragged. "You know what, Sam? You are a selfish jerk. All you ever think about is yourself. Yourself, and your stupid photo project."

Sam's head jerks upward and his parched mouth drops open.

"I know you lost your dad, and that sucks," Marco goes on. "It sucks in a way I can't understand. I know I don't know what that's like. But I know *all about* two years of taking care of *Sam*. Doing whatever *Sam* says. Going wherever *Sam* wants to get the next shot—waiting while he sets it up, being told what to do and sitting this way and that, putting up with his moods. When was the last time you did something for me?" Marco is leaning forward now. "Or asked me how I am? Or even thought about *me*, your supposed best friend, at all?"

Marco finishes talking and takes a step back. The tears and

frustration are gone from his face, replaced by uncertainty—like he just surprised himself.

Sam swallows hard. He had no idea his friend felt this way. His mind whirls. Should he have known, or guessed?

Probably.

Yes.

Still, he can't find any words. He has no idea what to say to Marco. Or even to himself. Everything feels unmanageably complicated.

"Sam!" a voice calls from behind. Sam turns and looks. His whole body lightens. Standing just twenty yards away is the most beautiful thing he has ever, ever seen: a set of purple scrubs with poodles on them.

Tears spring to his eyes. "Mom!" Sam hobble-runs into his mom's waiting arms. "Mom!" he says over and over while she wraps him into the tightest hug of his life. They hug and hug and hug, tears forming in their eyes, spilling down their cheeks.

She releases her grip, holding her son at arm's length. "When you weren't with the Nuñezes, I . . . I . . ." She fumbles on her words. "And when I heard Santa Bonita had burned . . ." Her voice is just a whisper, raspy and filled with the fear she also just lived through.

Sam's attention holds on the words *Santa Bonita burned*. Of course it did, and yet he hadn't known. Not for sure. "Mom, I left dad's camera in the village," he confesses. "It's probably . . ." Sam trails off.

"It's gone, Sammy." Sam's mom wraps her arms tighter around

her only child. "But *you* are here," she says, and in that moment Sam understands. The camera doesn't matter. The pictures don't matter. He can't bring his dad back and he can't freeze time. All he can do is appreciate what and who he has. Right now.

His eyes land on Marco over his mom's shoulder. Marco with his family. He will go over in a moment—he will hug them all. He will talk to his friend, say thank you and that he's so, so sorry. He will work on being a better friend . . .

Right after he finishes filling up on hugs from his mom.

CHAPTER
THIRTY-EIGHT

More French toast, boys?" Sam's mom turns away from the stove, three steaming pieces of egg-battered cinnamon-scented bread perched on a metal spatula. At her feet, Goodboy waits with his tongue out, hoping she might drop one.

Marco and Sam look up from the kitchen table at the crispy, steaming yumminess. Their plates are still smeared with butter and syrup from the last round, but they both nod eagerly.

Vivian puts a piece on each boy's plate and picks the last one up with her fingers. She takes a bite, eating it without putting anything on it, and tears off a small corner to "accidentally" drop for GB.

Marco and Sam quickly reload their toasts and then refocus their attention on the school newspaper that's spread out between them. The front-page article is Elsie's.

It's perfect Saturday morning reading. At least now that the evacuations are over, the sky is clearing, and most people are back in their homes. Or, in the case of Sam and his mom, in a new place.

When Sam first heard that their house had burned, with its darkroom and his dad's prints, with their computer and their dishes and their furniture and their clothes—their *everything*—he was still in shock from the whole experience. But it was not the numbness he'd felt when his dad died. Sam kept waiting for the grief to hit him again—kept waiting to *miss* all his stuff. But, weirdly, that feeling never really came. And though there's definitely stuff he wishes he still had, it doesn't hurt not to have it.

Sam's mom sprinkles blueberries on the boys' sticky toast and they lean in, shoulders touching, to read the article. Here in their cozy new apartment, closer to his mom's work, Sam has all he needs: his mom, his dog, his friend . . .

Falcon Creek Fire—The End or the Beginning?

The Falcon Creek Fire started near State Highway 21 and burned for 40 days. The blaze, believed to be started by dragging truck chains, was made worse by strong winds and a yearslong drought. Quickly becoming multiple fires, known as a "fire complex," it was described by all as "incredibly intense." It was just 63% contained after 20 days, when welcome autumn rains arrived to extinguish the portions that were too rugged for firefighters to reach. On Dec. 2, well over a month after it started, Falcon Creek Complex was at last pronounced extinguished.

The multifire complex left destruction in its wake:

Fifty-four thousand acres burned, including the village of Santa Bonita and three rural neighborhoods.

Forty-three buildings were destroyed

Marco puts a buttered finger on the line about buildings. "Do you think that includes your house, and Maverick's?" he asks.

Vivian nods. "It must include every house on our street, plus the homes on Orchard Road. But mostly the village."

Marco nods and the boys keep reading.

and 2,800 people evacuated. Twenty-three people, including 16 firefighters and 7 civilians, sustained nonfatal injuries. Additional losses included countless loss of animal wildlife and immeasurable destruction of natural habitats. Despite the damages and victims, all has not been lost and, in fact, there has been some renewal. Nature is made to survive.

As you read this, winter sunlight is reaching the forest floor, unhindered by shading branches. Tiny seedlings are getting ready to poke though blackened, nutrient-rich earth. Redwood seeds, released from their cones in the fire's blistering heat, are burrowing and preparing to sprout. Tiny insects, alerted by the fire's heat, are arriving in this renewing forest. They have traveled great distances to feast on partially burned plant matter. Birds, in turn, are flying in to feast on the flourishing insect population. By spring, when plants are truly springing to life, more creatures will begin to arrive. And by summer, small mammals will return to build new homes in the burn scar.

Fires, while devastating, bring new life. And unlike forest fires, which are invariably extinguished, life always, always goes on.

Sam forks the last bite of toast into his mouth and chews, thinking of Elsie's words. The cycles of nature are comforting, and though he *knows* that life will return, it's also true that things will never be the same. And sometimes, that's okay.

"Dude, are you done?" Marco nudges Sam's shoulder playfully and Sam snaps out of it. Yes, he's done, and for the day he is completely at Marco's disposal . . . or mercy depending on what Marco decides they are going to do. He owes his best friend *as many Saturdays as he wants* for coming back for him after he took off during the evacuation, and for being the *best* best friend. He was right—Sam had been acting like a selfish jerk. He was lucky that Marco stuck with him.

"So, what's it going to be? *Dragon Zone 3*? Matinee in Richland? You name it, I'm all yours!" Sam says, clearing their plates.

Marco smiles and reaches under the table to pat Goodboy. "How about we take GB to the beach?" he suggests.

Sam can hear GB's tail hitting the floor with a *thump, thump, thump* at the mention of his name and the beach. A winter beach walk with cool winds, soaring seabirds, lapping waves, and a frolicking dog sounds absolutely perfect.

"Dude!" Sam happily agrees.

CHAPTER
THIRTY-NINE

Sam's eyes dart back and forth as he watches the passing landscape out the window of his mom's car. The burn scar left by the Falcon Creek Fire whizzes past. Even though it's been a year, the damage is still very visible. Here and there on the blackened hills, he can see tiny hints of green, an unburned shrub, a small patch of sprouting grass, but mostly it is the scorched skeletons of trees . . . both standing and fallen.

At the top of the last ridge, before they can glimpse the ocean, the still-standing trees are silhouetted against a cloudless blue sky. The contrast is remarkable, and Sam holds up his new camera to capture it. He clicks the shutter, then takes the camera away from his eye to look at the screen beside the viewfinder. The image is there. Instantly.

"Did you get it?" his mom asks, glancing his way from the driver's seat. She's smiling. Her real smile. And Sam smiles back.

"Yup!"

With the money from their insurance, Sam and his mom have been able to replace what they need. In some cases, like the case of his new digital camera, they've even been able to upgrade.

The ribbing Sam endured when Marco first saw his Nikon D3500 had been totally worth it. Now there's no more darkroom developing. No more waiting. Mistakes are easily deleted, and sometimes, Sam has discovered, the mistakes are the shots he likes best.

Sam unrolls the window in the back seat so GB can hang his head out, and the family of three rides on in easy silence. It takes a little longer to get to the village than it used to, and Sam can't bike to school anymore—even with his new, proper-size Schwinn—but the trade-off has been worth it. Sam likes the smaller house his mom found for them to rent. It's closer to the hospital. Goodboy loves the fenced backyard, and they *all* love being home together now that his mom has stopped working nights. But even when his mom isn't there, it doesn't feel as lonely. Go figure.

As they turn into the village, Sam sits up straighter to see what's changed. Most of Main Street had burned down to nothing in the fire. By the time it got to the village, it was burning too hot and too fast to be stopped.

Though it's been a year, many blocks are mostly unrecognizable. Only about half the businesses that burned have managed to reopen. Fortunately, most of the others still plan to.

"Recovery takes time," Mr. Nuñez reminds Sam every time he sleeps over.

Happily, one of the first shops to reopen its tinkly door was Inside Scoop. Esther didn't waste a second rebuilding—it was like she knew Santa Bonita needed cold, creamy treats before anything else. Sam unrolls his own window and leans out, GB style, to view the brand-new sign hanging out front. It's shaped like a sugar cone, with two scoops balanced on top that Sam and Marco swear are chocolate and peanut butter.

Two doors down, the hardware store is still just a foundation, but Sam knows Hank has plans. Lucky for Hank, he decided to evacuate after all. His house, like the Durands', burned down to nothing—literally only a chimney remained. It was a lot of work to rebuild both a home *and* a business at the same time. Hank decided to focus on his house first.

The theater and bakery are back, too, and look remarkably similar to the way they did before. The only real difference is that the shrubs and flowers in the flower boxes are tiny compared to the well-established ones that burned.

Vivian takes a left and pulls into a nearly full parking lot. Miraculously, the large municipal park that sits at the end of their little valley didn't get burned at all. Sam's mom parks in one of the last open spots. "Here we are!"

Sam gets out first, then opens the back door and clips on GB's leash. "Ready for a party?" he asks the pup.

The picnic area is decorated with banners and signs:

REBUILD SANTA BONITA!
THANK YOU, FIRST RESPONDERS
SANTA BONITA: BETTER THAN EVER

Three double-long tables have been lined up for a buffet beside a row of cypress trees, and they're brimming with food. Goodboy drags Sam closer as Vivian adds a platter of hummus and veggies to the lot.

A trio of musicians is playing, and the sound of waves in the distance feels like it's keeping time. Sam's mom puts her arm around her boy's shoulders and they look at the green, grassy space. People mill and mingle all over. Some have spread out picnic blankets, others toss Frisbees or baseballs.

"Is that Elsie?" Sam's mom points to the blond girl by the swing set.

"Yup!" Sam says, nodding and heading over. Halfway there, Sam glances back to make sure his mom doesn't mind being abandoned so quickly. But she's smiling. Her friends are here, too, somewhere.

"Hey!" Elsie calls before bending down to help her little brother onto one of the swings.

Sam stops. He lifts the camera. *Click!* Got it.

"Nice!" Elsie approves the shot.

When Sam turns again, he spots Esther. He waves but she doesn't see him. She's brought her new Inside Scoop freezer cart to the party and is passing out custard cups for humans and pup cups for dogs. Sam's glad GB hasn't noticed yet because Esther is absolutely mobbed! Even with her niece, Zinna, working one side of the cart, they can barely keep up. Together they serve up cup after cup, their matching braids (Zinna's are still naturally dark) bobbing.

Sam raises his camera again. *Click!* He snaps the picture, capturing the laughter in both pairs of eyes.

With GB dictating the route, Sam and Elsie are pulled over to a cluster of picnic blankets laid out in the shade. People are bent into bridges, sitting cross-legged in a circle, and lying facedown in special chairs, taking advantage of the free yoga, meditation, and massage being offered. There's a lot of healing happening in Santa Bonita, but just as with the burn scar, there's still a lot of growth that needs to happen in the days ahead.

Goodboy keeps pulling, and Sam and Elsie keep following. It feels right to be gathering on the anniversary of the fire. Sam is glad the event has the vibe of a celebration and not a funeral. The smoke he smells is happily from a line of Weber grills covered in sizzling burgers and brats. Firefighters, including Gabi, are cooking up lunch. It smells delicious . . . and explains why GB is pulling so much.

"Sit, Goodboy," Sam tells his dog. He lifts his camera to line up a shot of a firefighter trying to accept a hug and flip a burger at the same time, when suddenly—

"Dude!" Marco sneaks up behind him and practically shouts the word in Sam's ear. He jumps but instantly starts laughing.

Surprisingly, Sam's anxiety has eased in the last year. Maybe because he finally figured out that some things really are out of your control!

Marco looks at the camera in Sam's hand and squints with one eye. "Hey, I thought you were done with that photo project!" he fake-pouts.

"I am. I swear!" Sam says, lifting his palm. "But come on, how about a quick selfie with my best model?"

"Flattery will get you everywhere." Marco beams and bats his eyelashes.

"Elsie, get in here!" Sam waves their other friend into the picture and holds the camera as high as he can, angling it toward the ground to get GB in the shot, too.

He clicks the shutter and looks at the screen.

"Dude!" Sam cracks up and whirls around to see Maverick lying on the grass behind them. Their classmate pulled off an epic photo bomb by sliding in next to GB and flashing a peace sign with impeccable timing!

Sam passes the camera around to share the picture and then hovers his finger over the delete button.

"Don't you dare!" Maverick interjects. "I need that," he says. "And since you guys stole my dad's Rubicon and got it incinerated, *you owe me*." He emphasizes the last three words and sounds downright ominous.

Sam's look clouds over. *Is he serious?*

No.

Maverick smiles and waves his hand, brushing off Sam's concern. "I'm just messing with you. It was an emergency, and we have insurance. Besides," he finishes, "it's just stuff."

Stuff. Marco and Sam exchange a look, then laughingly say in unison, "Yeah, it's just stuff."

FORTY

The young doe raises her head and stands stock-still in the autumn woods. Her burn scars are nearly invisible beneath her regrown fur, but they are there. At a little over a year, the deer is young enough that she would still be with her mother if she had survived the fire. Instead, she's all alone.

The doe listens intently to the sounds of the woods, knowing that predators are returning to her forest. Some of the coyotes, mountain lions, and bobcats that managed to flee have come back to the fertile hunting ground. Any one of them would like to eat her for supper. She waits, sensing the air around her, feeling the wind stir, the October sun warming her back. Then she slowly lowers her head and goes back to her grazing. There is always danger. But for the moment, she is safe.

ABOUT THE AUTHORS

Jane B. Mason lives in Carbondale, Colorado, where she spends her time writing, making jam, drinking tea, foraging wild edibles, cultivating her own vegetables, and swimming in all kinds of water. Her most recent titles, written with accomplice Sarah Hines Stephens, are the Rescue Dogs series and *Evacuation Order*. *Without Annette* was Jane's YA debut.

Sarah Hines Stephens lives in Oakland, California, where she likes to grow things, cook things, and walk with her dogs in the redwoods. When she is not writing books, Sarah sells books as a children's book agent and indie bookseller. It's a whole thing with her. Her most recent titles, written with her friend and coconspirator Jane B. Mason, are the Rescue Dogs series and *Evacuation Order*.